southern *devotion*

NEW YORK TIMES & USA TODAY BESTSELLING AUTHOR

KAYLEE RYAN

southern
devotion

1

Olivia

Standing in the corner of the room, I look around at my friends and family. My brother Mike and his new fiancée, Jamie, are smiling so big I fear their faces may crack open. I can't help but smile, too, when I think about my conversation with him earlier this week. He was actually worried she might say no. I mean, I get it. Asking someone to marry you is a big deal, but not with the two of them. They have a bond that tethers them together. Anyone who's near them can see it.

A year ago, I was worried about my big brother. He spent every spare minute at our family's bar, Mike's Tavern. I know he felt the pressure to keep the family business going, but he gave up a lot to do so. He and I took over a few years ago, although since he's met Jamie, I've moved into more than a bartender role. It's been good for both of us, me stepping up and him taking a few steps back. That first night I saw him with Jamie, it was obvious there was some type of connection. I couldn't be more thrilled at the way things turned out for them.

Strong arms wrap around me, and then his deep voice whispers in my ear. "Hey, Livy," David says, kissing my cheek.

David Johnson and I have been dating for a while now, a couple of years. He's good friends with my brother, Mike, and the rest of the guys in our clan, Aaron and Evan. He's been hinting that we need to move our relationship forward, but I've been hesitant. Not because of him; he's the best thing that has ever happened to me, and he owns my heart. No, my hesitation is all on me.

"We're next," he says, holding me a little tighter.

"You think so?" Of course, I already know the answer. If David had it his way, we would already be married and on our way to making our own family.

"I hope so," he says. "I want forever with you."

I melt against him, relishing the feel of his arms around me. I know one day he's going to get tired of waiting, and I don't want that to happen. When I look at my future, I see him in it. Of course, I do. There is no one else I would rather have by my side.

"They're happy," I say, looking at our friends and family. I turn to peer at him over my shoulder. "I love you."

His face softens. "I love you more. That's us, Livy." He motions his head to the room. "Nothing would make me happier than to make you mine."

"I'm already yours." The words are easy to say because they're true.

"Mine." He places a soft kiss just below my ear. "Mrs. David Johnson. Olivia Johnson," he whispers.

I close my eyes and let the idea of being his, taking his last name, wash over me. "I love the sound of that," I tell him honestly. I've been thinking about the future more lately, and without a doubt, he's the man for me.

"Then let's do it, baby. You tell me when and where, and I'm all over it."

I can't help but laugh. "We should go mingle."

"I'm wearing you down," he says with a kiss to the top of my head. He pulls away and laces our fingers together before leading me toward our family and friends. I don't know how many times in the last year we've had this conversation. I think back to the night that I confessed to my now-sister-in-law and our friends what my hesitation was. I work at Mike's, which is our family bar. My dad ran it before my brother, also named Mike, took over, and now it's just the two of us running things. Since he's met and fallen in love with Jamie, I've helped him more than just tending bar.

I confessed to them that I don't want to be the mom who works behind the bar. It never bothered me growing up, but kids can be cruel, and I want to do something that my children can be proud of. I've thought about it a lot since my slipped confession with the girls. I know what I do for a living shouldn't matter. I mean, it's not like I'm a stripper—not that there is anything wrong with that. It's just not for me.

I smile and laugh in all the right places, but the rest of the night, my mind races with all the reasons why I've been putting him off. At first, it was too soon. Not too soon to know I was in love with him, as that was immediate, but too soon for... well, I guess society's standards. We'd only been together a few months when he first told me he wanted to marry me. He didn't ask that time, but I still blew it off, not trusting his words. Over the time we've been together, there have been more moments like that than I can count. I always manage to change the subject, but he's serious. While he's never actually bent down on one knee and presented a ring, he would. I know that deep in my soul. If he thought for a second I would say yes, he'd do so in a heartbeat.

"Look at them," McKinley says from beside me.

Turning my head to look at her, I see she's grinning while watching Mike and Jamie. "I always thought it would have been you and Aaron."

"What?" My brows fly high, and I laugh.

"Come on, Liv, you had a crush on Aaron for years."

"He was one of my brother's best friends. It's like a rite of passage." I grin widely. "Besides, I ended up with the other best friend."

"Maybe so," she says with a chuckle. "I think you made the right choice." She motions to where David is standing with her husband, Evan, and her brother, Aaron. "He adores you."

"Good thing, because I don't plan on letting him go," I say, bumping my shoulder into hers.

"You know, I thought a lot about what you said that night. About not wanting to be the mom who works behind a bar."

I grimace. Is it too much to ask that my friends forget that conversation? "And?" I ask, needing to hear her thoughts on the matter, regardless of the unease I feel.

"And I get it, but I think you're wrong. That bar is your legacy. David has no problem with you working there. Let me ask you something. Growing up, were you ever embarrassed by your parents working in a bar?"

"Never," I say adamantly.

"There you have it. Stop worrying about what everyone else thinks and live for you." She places her hands over her growing baby bump.

"How you feeling?" I ask her, deliberately changing the subject.

"Good. It's kind of cool that Whit and I are just two months apart. I like that our kids are growing up together. Now, if we can get the newlyweds on board and get you and David down the aisle, and get to work on making babies, we'd all be able to say that about you, too." She winks.

"I do like the sound of that," I admit.

"Like the sound of what?" Whitney asks. She also has her hand over her even smaller baby bump.

"Yeah, we need details," Jamie chimes in.

"I was just telling Liv that Jamie and Mike need to get this wedding underway and start working on adding to our clan." She points to her belly. "And this one"—she points at me—"needs to stop letting fear and worry drive her, and say yes already so she can, too."

"Did he ask you again?" Jamie asks.

"Not technically, but it seems as though at least once a week he brings it up. More so since he found out Mike was proposing and these two" — I point to Whit and Kinley — "are expecting."

Jamie holds her hand in the air, showing off her engagement ring, her face alight with happiness. "You know you want one of these," she teases.

I easily admit, "I do."

Whitney reaches over and rests her hand on my arm. "Do you love him?"

"More than anything."

"Does he love you?" she asks.

"More than anything." I know where she's going with this, and my mouth turns into a smile.

"You have your answer. Stop worrying, and live, be happy," Kinley says.

I put my arm around her and Whitney, and they do the same to Jamie, bringing us all into a circle. "I love you, guys."

"We love you, too," they say in unison.

2

David

"Your place or mine?" I ask Olivia as we leave the restaurant.

With her head resting against the back of the seat, she turns to look at me. "Yours."

Reaching over, I take her hand and bring it to my lips. "You okay?" She got noticeably quiet toward the end of the party.

"Yeah." She smiles softly. "Just thinking."

"You want to talk about it?" If there's something bothering her, I want to know about it so I can fix it. There's nothing I wouldn't do for her.

"Nothing's wrong. Just processing the night, that's all."

"You girls looked like you were in deep conversation at one point."

"Just girl talk," she evades.

"I see how it is," I tease. Things with Olivia have always been easy. For years, I watched her, longed for her, really, not for the lack of looking like a pussy. I always thought she had a thing for Aaron, but when Aaron and Whitney got together, and she was fine with it, happy for them, I moved in. No way was I letting some other schmuck come in and take her from me. She's all I've ever wanted.

We ride to my place in silence, not uncomfortably so. She has something on her mind, and I want to give her time to work it out. She'll fill me in when she's ready. She always does.

"You ready for bed?" I ask as I pull into the driveway. My house is a two-story farmhouse. It's been completely remodeled, with a small pond out front and a big backyard. Perfect for a new family. It's why I bought it three months ago, and it is definitely not the house of a bachelor. Olivia's place is nice, too, just smaller and not with much yard space.

"I am." She places her hand over her mouth, covering a yawn. "Shopping wore me out." She laughs, climbing out of the truck.

She was part of the "keep Jamie away" plan while we set everything up at the restaurant for the engagement party. We all knew Jamie was going to say yes, though. All you have to do is look at the two of them together, and you can see it.

I meet up with her as we head up the steps. "What's holding you back, Liv?" I ask, reaching for her. She turns in my arms so she's facing me. I don't have to explain myself with my obscure question either. She knows exactly what I'm referring to. The truth is, I'm ready to start forever with her. Tonight, seeing all our friends happy and starting families… I want that.

She lifts her arms and places them around my neck. Looking into her eyes, I see her emotions. She's been running, evading, delaying… whatever you want to call it. Making excuses. "Surprise me," she whispers against my lips.

I pause momentarily in shock. "What?" I manage to ask when my brain reboots, my brows lifting. "I need you to replay that for me." I hold her a little tighter.

"Next time, surprise me." Her smile is soft, and I can see nothing but love in her eyes reflecting back at me.

"Olivia," I growl and pull her closer. "Don't tease me, beautiful." I need to make sure my mind isn't playing tricks on me. Is she really saying what I think she is?

"Surprise me," she repeats.

"You're ready?" I clarify. I've been asking her playfully to marry me since the beginning of our relationship. Every single time, she blows me off. I've never asked her straight up or on bended knee with a ring, the fear of her rejecting me too real. Something has been keeping her, keeping us from moving forward. I already have the ring. Hell, I've had it for close to a year now, waiting for the time I knew she was ready.

"I love you, David. I want the future we talk about. So next time, surprise me."

"We're doing this?" I confirm. I've waited for her to be on the same page as me for the majority of our relationship. I know she loves me. She just needed time. Time I was willing to give her. Not having her in my life wasn't an option.

"Yes." She clasps her hands behind my neck. After a few sweet kisses, she mumbles against my lips, "We're doing this," before kissing me again.

I want nothing more than to devour her, but I don't. I let her have this, let her control the pace while my mind races. I've had a lot of time to think about how I want to propose for real, so many different ideas. Now that it's here, I need to decide. None of them seems worthy of her.

"I love you," I say as soon as she pulls away.

"Mmm." She snuggles into my chest, too tired to offer more.

Unlocking the front door, I lead her inside before turning the lock back in place. We don't bother with lights as I guide her upstairs to the bedroom. We make our way to the attached bathroom and stand before the his-and-hers sinks, brushing our teeth. I love the nights she's here. When I bought this place, I wanted it to be ours, and it feels empty when she sleeps at her place. I made sure before purchasing it that she loved it. I can still remember the light in her eyes when I showed it to her before I made an offer. Without a doubt, I knew this was where we would live. Now more than ever before, I see it all play out in my mind—family dinners, playing with the kids in the backyard, sitting on the porch swing after the kids have gone to bed. All of it. In vivid detail, our future came to life, and my girl just informed me she's finally ready.

Now all I have to do is decide how and when. Shutting off the bathroom light, we head to bed. I strip down to my boxer briefs and toss my T-shirt to Liv. Then we crawl into bed. I pull her close, kiss her neck, and it seems like she's instantly asleep. Holding my future in my arms, I map out a plan.

My girl wants a surprise. She's going to get it.

3

Last night I told him to surprise me. I'm ready for our future. Ready to leave the worries behind and just be happy and live. I can still see his face, his shocked expression mixed with so much love. He truly is an amazing man, and I'm lucky he's chosen to give his heart to me.

Rolling over in his big king-size bed, I watch him sleep. His hands are under his pillow as he sleeps peacefully on his belly. His chocolate-brown hair, in need of a trim, is tangled from sleep. As I watch him, I let my mind wander to our future. This is where we'll be. I love this house, and he knows it. It's why he bought it. I'm sure of it. We'll need to put my place up for sale.

"What are you thinking about, gorgeous?" he asks, his voice laced with sleep.

"Living here," I tell him honestly.

"Yeah?" he asks, a little more alert. "You finally ready to move in with me?"

"As a matter of fact, I am," I confess.

This gets his full attention. He lifts his head, and his eyes bore into mine. "Don't tease me, Liv."

"I would never," I say in a tone hinting that he's offended me. The smile on my face tells him different.

"What's gotten into you? First last night, and now you're ready to move in? What changed?"

I don't even hesitate when it comes to my confession. "I used to think… well, it bothered me that I would be the mom who worked behind the bar. I know kids can be cruel, and I never wanted to be the reason my kids were made fun of or given a hard time. I thought I needed a career, a regular old nine-to-five job before we started the rest of our lives together."

His eyes soften. "Livy, you have a career. Mike's Tavern has been in your family for generations. It's a good thing you and your brother are doing, keeping the family business alive. You never need to feel less than for that."

"I know. It's my own stupid insecurities. I have this vision of the perfect life, with you, our kids, and it all fit. Everything… except for my job. I can see it all, from the wedding to when we're old and gray and sitting on the front porch, watching our grandkids play in the yard."

"Don't let what you fear others might say or think keep you from living your life, living this life with me." He leans in and kisses the corner of my mouth. "I love you, and your career doesn't have a damn thing to do with it."

"I know it was silly. I confessed to the girls a while ago, and they told me the same thing. Then last night, McKinley and I were talking, and it hit me. I'm keeping myself from living, letting fear hold me back." Reaching over, I brush his shaggy hair out of his eyes. "I love you, David, more than anything, and I'm sorry I've put you through this, put us through this. If I didn't let my fears get in the way, we would already be married and maybe even have a baby by now."

"Lots of babies." He nods.

"How many are we talking here, Mr. Johnson?"

"Well, we have four bedrooms here, and with the floor plan, it would be easy enough to add on." He grins.

"Let's start with three and go from there."

His lips brush against mine. "Three is a good number." He pulls away, and the smile on his face tugs at my heart. I've been holding us back for so long. I'm just glad he stuck around. "So, about this moving-in thing."

"Yeah, this place is bigger and ideal for a family."

"It is. We both agreed on that when I bought it. I've also asked you since the day I signed the papers to move in with me." He studies me closely. "You sure this is what you want?"

"Yes." No hesitation, no reservations. I'm ready for this, for him, for us.

"When?" he asks, sitting up. The sheet pools around his waist, and I can't help but run my eyes over his toned muscles, tanned from days in the hot sun.

"Is today too soon?" I ask.

His answer is pushing me back on the bed and kissing me deeply. I can feel the love, the happiness pouring off him. When he pulls back, his lips hover over mine. "You're really moving in?"

Regret washes over me. This man, so strong, kind, and loving, has given me all the space I need, and in doing that, I've made him uncertain of my feelings for him. He knows I love him, but my wariness has made him question that.

My hands cradle his cheeks. "Yes, I'm really moving in. I'll call the realtor tomorrow and get my place up for sale. I already have a lot of my clothes here. What furniture we don't want to bring, we can donate. I want nothing more than to live here with you, become your wife, have your babies, and live our happily ever after."

Again, a kiss. This time, he crushes his lips against mine, pushing his tongue past my lips, taking what he wants, celebrating the fact that I'm no longer fighting him. "Call your parents and tell them we can't make it to dinner," he says.

"What?" I laugh. "Why not?"

"Because we're moving you in." He beams down at me.

My heart swells at the happiness radiating from him. "How

about we go over and start packing. We can still go to Mom and Dad's for dinner, and afterward, we can load up your truck and bring the first load over here."

"How about I call Mike, Aaron, and Evan, have them bring their trucks, and we load up all four of them and bring them over?" he counters.

I chuckle. "Dave, I have to pack. It's going to take time."

"Fine," he grumbles. "But as of today, you sleep here. So make sure you have the essentials, because you are in this bed every night from here on out."

"Deal," I agree, and we seal it with a kiss.

4

David

We're sitting at my future in-laws' around the dining room table. Dinner plates are long gone as we sit and talk about a little bit of anything and everything. I want to shout it out that Liv is finally moving in with me, but I hold it in. We rushed through breakfast and went straight to her place, stopping at the bar for boxes on the way. We managed to pack up her entire master bathroom and most of her clothes. There are still some left hanging in the closet that we're just going to leave on the hangers and toss in the back seat of the truck.

I can't help but watch the clock, waiting for it to be time to leave so we can load up the boxes and take them home, to *our* home. The one I bought in hopes I would one day be calling it just that. My home with her.

"Dinner was great, Mom, as always," Olivia says. "We need to get going."

"No need to rush off," her dad chimes in.

"Well, we kind of have some boxes to move."

Reaching under the table, I lace her fingers through mine. This is happening. She's telling her parents. I'm not just dreaming a very vivid dream. My girl is finally coming home. Suddenly, every hope I've had for us is starting to fall into place.

"Boxes?" her mom asks, confused.

"Yeah." She looks over at me and smiles softly. I want to lean in and press my lips to hers, but instead, I give her hand another gentle squeeze under the table. "I'm moving in." She turns back to her mom.

"Finally!" her mom cheers, and everyone starts laughing.

I've known the Wallace family my entire life, having grown up here. I've already talked to her parents and her brother. They know where I want this to go with us. They also know I've been trying to get her to move in for three months, since the day I bought the house. "Finally," I agree.

"You need some help?" Mike offers.

"Oh, we can all help," her mom adds.

"Actually, we have my bathroom and bedroom all packed up. We just need to load the boxes. I'm going to call the realtor tomorrow and set up a time to get mine on the market."

"I'll swing by and help you load," Mike tells me.

"And we"—Jamie smiles at Olivia—"can start packing the other rooms."

Liv throws her head back and laughs. "I didn't realize y'all would be so eager to help me move."

They all laugh, and it feels right. These people are going to be my family. I'm grateful to have such a great relationship with them, and that they accept me in their daughter's and sister's life. Mike and I are friends, and from day one, I've never held back how I feel about his sister. Out of all of them, he knows how big a deal this is to me. To have her with me, under the same roof.

With a round of hugs and handshakes, we say our goodbyes, with Mike and Jamie following us to Olivia's old place. Mike and I get to work loading the already packed boxes in my truck while the girls start packing more.

"You ready to pop the question?" Mike asks.

"Damn right, I am."

"You still have the ring?"

I whip my head around to look at him. "Of course, I do. What kind of question is that?"

He shrugs, and I can tell he's fighting a smile. "You've had it for a damn long time," he reminds me.

"I know that. She wasn't ready. I didn't want to rush her or risk her saying no. I'm only asking one woman to marry me on bended knee, and I needed to know she was ready."

"I've heard you ask her," he says.

"On bended knee," I remind him. "I've teased and asked jokingly, waiting for her to give me a sign that she's ready. Last night, all of a sudden, she was ready. Then this morning, she shocks me further by telling me she wants to move in. I feel like I hit the fucking lottery," I say with a laugh and slam my tailgate shut.

"I bet you do. You know how you're going to ask her?"

"Man." I take my hat off my head, run my fingers through my hair, and put it back. "I've thought about it a million times. I have so many ideas, and I just need to decide on one."

"I would have thought it was all planned down to the minute." He laughs.

"I want it to be special, you know? I've asked her so many times, gauging her reaction, and when I really do it, when I present her with the ring, it needs to be more."

"I think you're overthinking it."

"This from the guy who went all-out on his proposal."

"You got me there. Let me know if I can do anything to help. No way could I have pulled my plan off without all of you, the girls especially."

"Thanks, man. I'm still letting it sink in that she's moving in with me, and that after all this time, she's ready. I'm afraid I'm dreaming."

He laughs at my expense. "It's real, my man. She loves you. Always has. Olivia has always marched to the beat of her own drum. Stubborn as a mule, but you and I both know she's as soft-hearted as they come."

"That she is. Thanks, man. I'm going to take a few days and enjoy the fact that this is finally happening for us. Then I'll dive into planning."

"Let me know," he says just as the girls walk up.

"Let you know what?" my ever-nosy future fiancée asks.

"Aaron and Evan were thinking of planning a day to take the RZRs out. I told him to let me know when."

"Oh, is this a guys-only thing? It's been forever since we've all been out riding."

"Yes," Mike speaks up before I have a chance to.

I'm digging myself into a hole and am now going to need to call Evan and Aaron and warn them. We might as well plan a day to ride while we're at it. It's been a hell of a long time since we've been riding.

"Thanks for your help." I hold my fist out, and he bumps his into mine.

"Anytime. You"—he points to his sister—"get the rest packed up, and we'll come back this weekend."

"A week?" she asks, as if we're telling her she has to go through fifty years of possessions.

"Can you not handle a week?" he asks.

"Pfft. I did all this in a day. I'll be ready," she assures him.

"Great. I've got the bar covered, so if you need to take a couple of days this week to get things ready, have at it."

"Thank you. I just might do that," she says, squaring her shoulders.

We're all shocked at her reply. She never misses work and rarely asks for help with anything.

I snake my arm around her waist and pull her into me. "This is happening," I whisper in her ear.

"Yeah." She looks up at me. "It is."

Leaning down, I kiss her forehead. If this is a dream, I don't ever want to wake up.

5

Olivia

The morning sun is poking just above the trees. I've been lying here for the last hour, watching its slow rise through the window of David's bedroom. Scratch that, *our* bedroom. It's hard to explain how I feel now that we're finally moving forward in our relationship. It's something I've always wanted, but I've foolishly let my insecurities hold me back. Hell, I don't even know where they came from. I do that sometimes, get in my own head. I'm glad I opened up to my girls, and they were able to get through to me. Sure, more than likely, I would still be here in this bed, but it would be his bed, not ours. There's a lightness in my chest from that simple fact alone.

He knows I'm ready, that I'm no longer going to hold back from what I want. I'm lucky as hell that he's put up with me this long, but that's David. He's honest, kind, and has the patience of a saint. And he's all mine.

"Morning, Livy," he whispers, kissing my neck.

"Morning." I lace my fingers through his hand that's resting against my belly, holding me to him.

"This is our new normal. We wake up, go to work, and then you come home to me. To our home." He kisses my shoulder.

"So I'm not crazy thinking this all feels new?"

"It's new for us. This is the beginning of forever. We both knew that's where we were headed — at least, I think we did — but now we're making it happen. I can't tell you how happy I am that you're living here with me. That this is our home."

"I'm ready," I whisper. David is a smart man. I'm sure he knows what I'm saying. Yes, I'm ready for the rest of our lives together, but I'm also ready to say yes. He just needs to ask me again. I know he's trying to plan some elaborate proposal. That's David, always trying to make things special for me. It's not necessary, but I love him more for the thought alone.

"I called Aaron and Evan last night. I'm off for the next two days. You think we can get you moved in all the way, everything of yours and mine under this roof by then?" he asks.

I roll over and run my hands across his five o'clock shadow. "Yeah, I think we can manage that. Look what we did in just a few hours yesterday."

"Wanna know a secret?" he asks, kissing the corner of my mouth.

"Always." I nod.

"I want to do it fast for so many reasons. One is because this is what I've wanted since the day I put in the offer. You, living here with me, us making this place our home. I also don't want to give you the chance to change your mind. Not that I think you're going to. It's just that I've wanted this, us, and you've been less than enthusiastic about us moving forward. I know you love me, but I wasn't sure this would ever happen for us," he confesses.

"I'm sorry, babe. I'm so damn lucky you've put up with me all this time. It was never you. It was never that I didn't love you or want all the things we talked about. I was scared."

"You're not scared anymore?" I hear the worry in his voice.

"I'm not. Do you want to know why?" I ask, and he nods. "Because, David Johnson, I know that no matter what life throws at us, you are going to be right there by my side. I know you will catch me when I fall, and if my job becomes an issue, we will work it out together. I know you are going to be the best husband and father a family could ask for." I place my hand on his chest over his heart. "Because I know this beats for me just as mine beats for you. Nothing can break that."

"I fucking love you," he says, capturing my lips with his.

After a few sweet kisses, I reluctantly pull away. "We have packing to do."

"We do, as soon as I make love to you in our bed."

"Really?" I laugh, tilting my head to the side to allow his lips to roam. "It's not like that's never happened in this bed before."

"It was never *our* bed before yesterday. We were exhausted last night, but today, *today* I'm ready to take you on every solid surface in this place. Our place," he says, nipping at my ear.

"I think I can get on board with that, but then my house won't get packed up, which will delay the realtor, which delays this being the only home I have." I know my words will do the trick.

"Fine, not every surface, just the bed." He reaches over and grabs a condom from the nightstand. "You ready to give these up yet?" he asks.

"Actually, yes."

He freezes. He's naked, sitting back on his knees between mine, staring down at me with a look of pure love and, right now, shock on his face. "Liv, baby, are you feeling okay?"

I can't stop the smile from tilting my lips. "I let my fears control me for too long. They were irrational and unwarranted. If I were to have your baby, it would be the greatest blessing," I tell him. "Besides, I'm on the pill."

"Yeah, but that's not changed since we've been together."

"No, you're right. But I have. I know it doesn't matter what my career is. What I do for a living will not define me as a wife and mother. Working at Mike's Tavern is not something to be ashamed of. Honestly, I'm embarrassed that I let my irrational worries keep us from moving forward."

"You sure about this?" he asks, holding up the condom.

"I've never been more sure about anything. I don't want anything between us the first time we make this bed ours," I say, reaching out and gripping him.

He tosses the condom on the floor and pulls my hand away from him. "Just the thought of being inside you bare has me ready to lose my shit, Liv. I can't have you touching my cock, not right now," he says, gripping my hips and pulling me into him. "You sure?" he repeats, and I nod. I watch him as he grips his length and guides himself inside of me slowly, inch by delectable inch, until he's fully seated. "Holy fuck," he breathes. His eyes are closed tightly, his grip on my hips strong, almost painful, but the smile on his face? I can't look away.

I can't take my eyes off him as he bites down on his lip. It's a heady feeling to know it's me who's causing this reaction from him. Lifting my hips, he slides in just a little deeper, and a moan falls from his lips.

"Dave, I need you to move." I lift my hips again to prove my point.

His eyes open and lock on mine. "I love you, Olivia." He pulls out and slowly dives back in. "You're so hot wrapped around my cock." He pulls out and thrusts back in a little faster this time. "So wet." Again, faster with each stroke. "I can feel your pussy squeezing me, so fucking soft," he murmurs as his thrusts grow faster.

All I can do is hang on for the ride. I slide my arms under his and sink my nails into his back, which seems to spur him on even further.

Leaning in, he captures my lips in a searing kiss, saying everything that neither one of us can find the words to express.

"I'm close," he pants against my lips. "Are you with me, baby?"

"Y-yes," I say, digging my nails a little deeper as I feel the rush of electricity flowing through my veins.

"Come with me," he demands, and that's all it takes for me to crash into a world of oblivion. It's pure bliss as wave after wave of ecstasy rolls through me. When the final one hits, I wrap my arms around him, holding him to me, not ready to lose our connection just yet.

"Open those eyes, Livy. I need to see you." With extreme effort, I force my lids open to find him watching me, his face hovering over mine. "There's my girl," he says, kissing me sweetly. "Life-altering, Liv."

"For you, too?" I ask.

He chuckles. "Making love to you always brings me to my knees, just being inside of you. But making love to you bare, that's a whole nother level." He presses his lips to mine yet again. "I feel like I'm a part of you."

"You are." I cup his face. "You're my heart, David, always have been. I'm sorry I've been distant and holding back. No more, I promise. I want everything we've talked about. Marriage, kids, the life we've dreamed, it's going to come true. I'll make sure of it."

His reply is to bury his face in my neck. "I don't want to pull out. I don't want to lose this feeling."

"I'm yours," I tell him, running my fingers through his hair. "This is our new reality, babe." We hold each other for what feels like hours, when actually it's mere minutes. "We really need to shower and start packing up my stuff."

"Yeah." He lifts his head to look at me. "You go first, and I'll make us some breakfast."

"You're not joining me?"

"Baby." He smiles. "You and I both know that if I don't pull myself away from you and walk downstairs, we won't be leaving this house today. Go shower, and I'll cook. Then tonight, we're doing this again," he says, kissing my lips and slowly easing out of me.

I can feel him, us. It's messy but so worth it. "You get this," I say, ignoring the mess we made, "for the rest of your life."

"No sweeter words have ever been spoken." He climbs off the bed and pulls on a pair of shorts.

"Aren't you going to, you know, clean up?" I ask.

"Nope. I want you, us, all over me while I make you breakfast. Go"—he nods toward the bathroom—"before I change my mind and we stay in this bed all day."

"We could do that, you know," I offer, because that sounds like a damn good idea.

"We could, but I want you here. All of you, all of your stuff. And being buried balls deep inside you all day, no matter how appealing the thought of staying now, won't get me that result." With that, he turns and exits the bedroom.

Making a mental note to wash the sheets, I climb out of bed and head toward the shower. Today feels like the first day of the rest of our lives. I can't wait to see what the future holds.

6

David

Reaching into the bed of my truck, I grab the last box Olivia just shoved my way. "This is it," I tell her, even though she already knows.

"I can't believe we got my entire house packed up and moved in two days."

"Well, you're donating most of your furniture," I remind her.

"I know, but still… you're one determined man, David Johnson."

"You're damn right," I agree with her. She gave me the green light I've been waiting for.

"Let me get this in the house, and then we can go back and do one final walk-through. Make sure there's nothing you missed or decide you want to keep."

"Not a bad idea, although I'm pretty positive we got everything."

"The Salvation Army is coming by tomorrow to pick up what's left."

"They are?"

"That's what you wanted, right?" That's what she said, but it's a possibility she's changed her mind.

"Yes, that's what I wanted. I just didn't realize that you called them already."

"I did it this morning. After the progress we made yesterday, I knew we would be finished today."

"Two days." She laughs. "You are one determined man."

Leaving the box on the open tailgate, I reach up and place my hands on her hips, lifting her from the back of the truck. Instead of letting me set her feet on the ground, she wraps her legs around my waist. "You, my love, were just as focused as I was."

"Mm-hmm," she murmurs, kissing my neck.

It's on the tip of my tongue to ask her to marry me; it's something I would have done a week ago. Now, everything is different. I know she's ready, and no way am I willing to risk her thinking me saying the words is her true proposal. My girl deserves the fairy-tale proposal she's always wanted.

What she doesn't realize is that I know her better than she thinks I do. I've known for years that she wants the fairy tale. The romantic proposal and the country wedding. I think her fears stem from worrying that her dream proposal and wedding would not live up to her reality, and she'd be disappointed. My girl loves her Disney movies. She thinks it's because of the job at the bar, but I know better. She's worried she's not going to get her dream. I'm just a small-town boy. I work on the ranch with both Aaron and Evan. When they teamed up, they brought me on board. I work hard for what I have, and that includes Olivia. I'll never stop showing her what she means to me, and I'll make certain she gets her dream proposal and wedding. Besides, all I've ever dreamed of is her. She's given me my dream; the least I can do is give her hers.

"You're my dream," I tell her.

Her eyes shimmer with tears. "I love you." She buries her face in my neck, and I hold her tightly.

The honking of a horn has us pulling apart. When I look over my shoulder, I see Mike and Jamie pulling into the drive.

"Hey, you two. Need some help?" Jamie asks.

"This is the last one," Liv tells her as I set her back on her feet.

"You packed up your entire house in two days?" Mike asks.

"Well, technically, it was three days, if you count what we did on Sunday."

"Determined." Jamie laughs.

"You're damn right," I agree.

I hear a woof and notice Mike is holding their puppy, the one I went with him to pick up. "Hey, little guy," I say, rubbing his head.

"Oh my God! He's so cute. The picture you showed me doesn't do him justice. What did you name him?" Liv asks Jamie.

"Ace."

"Aww, Dave, we need a puppy," she says, cooing at the little furball in her brother's arms. "Can I hold him?" Mike hands him over. The puppy settles in her arms, closing his eyes.

"He likes to snuggle," Jamie tells her.

She looks over at me and smiles. "He's too cute."

"You really want one?"

She seems to think about my question before her eyes meet mine. "We talked about a dog for the kids to play with," she says, as if it's just the two of us.

"Kids?" Mike and Jamie ask at the same time.

"Not yet." She shakes her head and laughs. "We're getting there."

I want to drop to my knees and beg her to be mine. I can run in the house and get the ring, and make it official. Then we can start on those babies. But I don't. I need it to be her dream proposal, then wedding, and then the babies. However, the dog...

we can make that happen now. "We did," I say, agreeing with her earlier statement. "We can get a dog."

"Where did you get him?" she asks Mike.

He points to me. "This guy found him for me. They have more." He smiles.

"Can we go?" she asks.

"Now?"

"Yes, now." Her eyes are bright with excitement.

Pulling my phone out of my pocket, I scroll through my contacts until I find the number for the lady Mike bought Ace from. "Hey, Susan, this is David Johnson. I was wondering if you have any puppies left?" Liv's eyes find mine as she waits for a signal from me. "Great, can we stop by in about thirty minutes or so? My future wife fell in love with the one her brother bought." Liv's eyes widen when I say 'future wife.' It's the first time I've mentioned it since she told me she was ready. "Great. We'll see you soon." I end the call and slide my phone back into my pocket.

"Well?" she asks.

"She has three left. One male and two females. I'm sure you heard me tell her that we would see her tonight?"

She turns to her brother and Jamie. "Sorry, but we've gotta go." She hands the puppy off to Jamie and grabs my hand, pulling me toward the truck, causing us all to burst out laughing.

"Let me get this last box in the house, and then we can go."

"Fine," she says, reaching for the passenger door. "Hurry up." She climbs into the cab and shuts the door.

"You've got your hands full with her." Mike laughs.

"I wouldn't want it any other way."

We say a quick goodbye before I grab the last box and carry it to the attached garage. I set it with the others, and my lips tilt with a smile. She's here. All of her stuff is here. Now I need to focus on the proposal. I want her to have my last name sooner rather than later. We've waited long enough to start the next phase of our lives together.

7

Olivia

"What should we name her?" I ask David on our way to the pet supply store.

"I thought you had a name in mind already?" He glances over at me with the puppy in my arms before returning his eyes to the road.

"I do, but she's ours, so I want your opinion."

"Okay, so let's hear it."

"I was thinking Dixie, or maybe Lucy." I pet the sleeping ball of fur in my arms.

"Dixie Johnson, Lucy Johnson, either works," he says after adding his last name to both.

"Wallace hyphen Johnson," I say, just to see his reaction.

We pull into the parking lot, and he puts the truck in Park before turning in his seat to look at me. "You plan on hyphenating your name?" he asks. He sounds disappointed.

"You okay with that?" I counter.

I watch as he processes my question. "Yes. I mean, when I imagine it, it's always just Olivia Jean Johnson, but it's your choice if you want to hyphenate."

"You're an amazing man, David Johnson. The thought of hyphenating my name has never crossed my mind. I was just joking with you about the dog. Olivia Jean Johnson has a great ring to it."

"Yeah?" he asks, hopeful.

"Yes. Now, it's time to get this little thing some toys and food and a bed and whatever else we happen to find." I laugh.

"So, her name is…?" he asks.

"Dixie. I like Dixie."

"Welcome to the family, Dixie," he says, gently running his large hands over her tiny head.

Butterflies dance inside my belly at the mention of us being a family. I want us to be official. I almost remind him again that I'm ready, but I told him to surprise me. Although patience is not my strong suit, I know I need to be just that: patient. He's waited forever for me to come to terms with where our future is going. I can give him time, all the time he needs. Regardless, he's mine, and I'm his, and now this little furball, Dixie, is ours.

Nearly two hours later, we're loading the truck with our purchases. I went a little overboard, but she needed a bed, some toys, food, treats, a collar, a leash, and they had these cute little sweaters. I had to get her one in pink, and then I happened to see one in blue and picked it up for Ace.

"You do know she's going to be a big dog, right?" David asks on our way home.

"Yeah, and?"

"The sweater?"

"It was too cute to pass up. She's tiny now and will look adorable. Besides, you have to get them used to that kind of thing when they're small."

"So you plan on dressing her up all the time?" He tries to hide his laughter.

"Maybe," I say, snuggling Dixie a little closer. "Hey, can we swing by Mike and Jamie's so I can give them the sweater I got for Ace? Oh my gosh, they're siblings. I bet they miss each other."

I feel sad for the pups who have been pulled away from their momma and brothers and sisters.

David reaches over and places his hand on my thigh. "Yeah, baby, we can stop."

I settle back in my seat and realize that not only am I happy, happier than ever, but I'm content. I wasted so much time. I can't wait to see what the future holds for us.

"Aww," Jamie says as I climb out of the truck with Dixie in my arms. "Look at her."

"They're brother and sister," I remind her. I'm not sure what it is about these little balls of fur that turns my heart inside out.

"That's right." She nods. "Is she going to be an inside or outside dog?"

I look over at a grinning David.

"Whatever you want, baby." He chuckles.

"She's too tiny to be outside."

"That's what this one said," Mike says, pointing at Jamie.

"Hey." She hip-checks him, both of them grinning like fools.

"We got Ace a present," I say, handing her the sweater.

Jamie turns to look at Mike. "See, I told you it was a good idea." She turns back to face me. "He said, 'Babe, dogs don't like sweaters,' but what do you know?" she teases him, her voice turning back to her own.

"Good impression." I laugh.

"Hush it," Mike says, grinning.

I watch as the two of them have some type of silent conversation, and my heart swells for my big brother and my friend.

"So," Jamie says, "do you all have plans two weekends from now?"

I look over at David, who shakes his head. "Not that I know of. I'll probably still be unpacking boxes," I laugh.

David steps up behind me and places his hands on my hips. "It's my life's mission to get you unpacked and settled," he whispers only for me before kissing my cheek.

"We're thinking about a trip to the Florida Keys. My parents are there for a few weeks. We thought it would be fun to get everyone together, take a big family trip," Jamie says, her eyes smiling.

"Uh-huh, what are you hiding from me?" I ask, studying her.

She looks over at my brother, and he gives her a subtle nod. "We're getting married!" She jumps up and down with poor little Ace's head bobbing with her. "We didn't want to wait, and my parents are there, and yours said they would come… and a small beach wedding to seal the deal is all we want."

"Seal the deal?" I ask her.

"Yeah, all that really matters at the end of the day is that we're married."

"Don't you want the wedding you've always dreamed of?" I ask her. It's romantic, but I've had the same vision for my wedding since I was a little girl.

"I never really dreamed of the wedding as much as the man whom I would call my husband. I wanted the kind of love that consumes you and makes you whole at the same time. That's all I need."

My brother wraps his hand around the back of her neck and pulls her into a kiss.

"So, in two weeks you're going to be my sister?" I ask once he sets her free.

"Yes. We're not really doing a wedding party. We're going to invite Aaron and Whit, and Evan and Kinley, but we're not sure they'll be able to make the trip. But you two, we need you two there."

"We'll be there," David assures her. He then holds his hand out for my brother to shake.

Just like that, we're the last remaining holdouts. Not because we're not ready, but because I've been irrational at best and let fear cloud what has been right in front of me all along. Turning in his arms, I hug him tightly, hoping he gets the message. *I love you, and I'm sorry for putting you through so much.*

We say our goodbyes with the promise to book our flights. On the way home, I can't help but wonder if I waited too long. Maybe he's over asking me. I can't say that I would blame him.

8

David

She was quiet on the drive home, then disappeared upstairs to take a shower. I took Dixie out on her leash, which she seems to hate, before bringing her back inside and using the baby gates we bought to barricade her in the kitchen. I set up her bed and some puppy pads, which the store associate, who could not have been a day over sixteen, assured us worked like a charm. With Dixie sleeping soundly in her big, comfy bed, I check to make sure the door is locked, turn out the lights, and head upstairs. If I'm lucky, Olivia will still be in the shower, and I can join her.

"Damn," I say when I see her walking out of the bathroom into our room. She's already wearing one of my T-shirts. "I was hoping to shower with you."

"Yeah? You want me to go back in?" She smirks, pointing over her shoulder.

"This works, too." I take a few large steps to reach her, wrapping my arms around her waist and pulling her into me. "You okay?"

"Of course," she says way too quickly.

"Livy." I wait for her to raise her head and look at me. "What's going on in that pretty head of yours?"

She heaves a heavy sigh as she pulls away and takes a seat on the bed. "I always knew I loved you. That was never a question. I knew you loved me, and I wanted all the plans we talked about. I'm mad at myself," she confesses.

I have a feeling I know where this is going and hate that she's still beating herself up over this. It's done, and we're moving forward. That's all that matters. I open my mouth to tell her that, but she beats me to it.

"I hate it, Dave. I hate that I put us through that. That I made us wait. We should be married by now, maybe thinking about a baby, if not already having one on the way. Instead, here we are, me just now moving in, and we're not even engaged."

"Hey." I smile, letting her know I'm teasing, trying to lighten the mood. "I've asked multiple times." I grin.

Her face falls. "I know." Her voice is thick with emotion.

"Baby, listen to me. I've never asked you on one knee. I knew you weren't ready for that, and honestly, I couldn't stand the thought of you telling me no in that situation. That doesn't mean that every time I asked you wasn't coming from deep in here." I place my hand over my chest, covering my heart. In just a few more strides, I'm grabbing her hands and tugging her to the edge of the bed. Her legs open automatically, allowing me to step between her thighs. "I'm only doing it once, Liv. There will be one time that I get on bended knee and ask the love of my life to marry me. There is only one love of my life, and that's you," I say, kissing the corner of her pouty lips. "It's always been you. You told me you were ready, and to surprise you. Is that still what you want?"

"Of course, it is," she says, trying to fight against the tears that are welling in her eyes.

"That's what I'm going to do. I want it to be special for both of us. I'm only ever going to do it once in my life, so I have to get it just right."

"You don't know that," she counters. "What if something happens to me and you get remarried?"

I place my index finger over her lips to stop her from saying more. "Don't think like that. We have to live for today, and today, all I see is you. I can't even imagine a day of my life without you in it. We can't let the what-ifs and the fears of the world guide us. Just this," I say, this time placing my hand over her heart. "This heart of yours is mine, Olivia Wallace. You gave it to me, and I intend to keep it."

She looks up at me with those sparkling green eyes, and I'm tempted to rush to the safe in the office and get her ring, but I don't. Instead, I hold her stare, willing her to trust in this and our love for one another.

"I love you," she whispers.

"I love you, too." I can't wait another minute to kiss her, so that's exactly what I do. Pressing my lips to hers, I take my time tasting as she mimics the motion, and our lips move in perfect harmony.

Pulling away from the kiss, I rest my forehead against hers. "Anything else you want to talk about?" I ask.

"I wish it were us," she murmurs. "I wish it were us who were getting married in two weeks."

"Me, too, baby. We'll have our day. You'll get your outdoor country wedding that you've always dreamed of."

"So you do listen?" She laughs softly.

"Every fucking word, Liv. There's nothing that passes these lips that I don't capture up here." I point to my head.

"What about you? What kind of wedding do you want? This isn't all about me, you know."

"You really want to know?" I ask her. She nods. "My ideal wedding is one where you, my beautiful Olivia, are walking down the aisle toward me. Nothing else matters, as long as at the end of the day, you're my wife." She offers me a sweet smile. "Now, let's talk about this shindig," I say, pulling back the covers and motioning for her to climb under. Once she's settled, I pull my shirt over my head and kick off my jeans.

"What about Dixie?"

"She's fine. I took her out and barricaded her in the kitchen." I climb in next to her and burrow under the covers. "Now, tell me how it's going to go down."

"My dream wedding?"

"Nope. *Our* wedding. Tell me how it's going to be."

"Summer, early fall. Outside. I picture it being in a field of flowers. Not a huge event, just those closest to us."

"I thought you wanted a huge country wedding?"

"I never said huge." She laughs. "But country, yes. That's us, and I want the day to encompass who we are and who we'll be together as much as possible."

"So, something outside, in a field of wildflowers, with our closest friends and family. What else?"

"My bouquet will be pink and white roses, with some wildflowers mixed in. I don't really want a big wedding party. I think it's ridiculous to have them spend money on clothes they'll never wear again. My dress… well, it's simple, yet elegant."

"Tell me more," I say, pulling her close.

"Nope. That's a surprise. Besides, I've never even seen the perfect dress. It's just an idea in my head."

"I think you should start looking. Doesn't that sort of thing take time?"

"Yeah, I mean it can, but we're not even engaged," she says hesitantly.

"Oh, we are. You're going to be my wife. My ring's not on your finger yet, but that's a technicality. What you described sounds pretty simple, minus the dress. Start looking."

"You're serious?"

"Yes." I place a kiss on her temple.

"Okay," she agrees; however, I can tell from the tone of her voice that it's reluctantly. "It's just weird to not be officially engaged and shopping for a wedding dress."

"Trust me, Liv."

"Okay."

"Now, what about a reception?"

"I thought just some tables set up under a white tent, or Mom and Dad have the old barn out back behind their house that they use for storage. We could clean it up and set up a few tables, string some lights. A small cake, some homemade pork barbecue with some sides."

"You have a field of wildflowers in mind?" I ask her, knowing she does. We've ridden the horses and the four-wheelers through that field many times over the years, both before she was mine and after.

"Yeah, you know the one in the back of the property at Mom and Dad's?"

"That's always been your favorite spot."

"It's beautiful there. I can imagine the pictures of us in the field of wildflowers." She snuggles closer, burying her face in my chest.

"It's pretty far back on the property."

"It is, but with just close friends and family, we can get them back there. Hell, they don't have to dress up, and we can take them back on a hay wagon. Can you imagine Lexi and Walker? They would love it."

"They would," I agree. "So that's it? That's all it takes to make the day special for you?"

"No. It's you, that's what makes it special. The rest just paints the picture of the love we share."

"Very poetic." I chuckle.

My laughter dies out, and we lie there, letting the silence surround us. It's not uncomfortable, not with her here in my arms and not with the subject at hand. We just planned our wedding. Well, she did, but I meant it when I said all I needed was her.

"What about me?" I ask her. "What am I wearing?"

She laughs softly. "I say some nice jeans, a button-down, and your cowboy boots."

"No monkey suit?"

"Nope."

"You really do love me," I say dramatically, causing us both to laugh.

That's how we drift off to sleep—her in my arms, and laughter and love surrounding us.

9

Olivia

David was gone this morning when I woke up. It's Saturday, but he told Evan and Aaron he would help with a couple of new horses that were being delivered today. He said that was the least he could do because they let him off to help me move. It is, but I don't like waking up without him. I knew he was going, but I wish he had woken me up before he left.

Speaking of David… I look down at my cell that's ringing, his picture flashing on the screen.

"Hey," I greet him.

"What are you getting up to today?" he asks.

"Thought about unpacking some boxes."

"Why don't you call one or all of the girls and go dress shopping? I can help you unpack. I don't want you lifting all those boxes."

"Can you hear me rolling my eyes?" I sass.

He laughs. "Really. You know Mike is at the bar, getting ready for tonight. I'm sure Jamie would love to get out of the house."

"What about Dixie?"

"Leave the baby gates up, and she'll be fine in the kitchen."

"I guess I can call her. I still feel weird about this." I know we're going to do it, but it feels presumptuous, even if we are both on the same page.

"Don't. It's happening, Livy." His voice is solid, strong, and I have zero doubt that he means it.

"I missed you this morning," I tell him instead of acknowledging his "It's happening" comment.

"You looked too peaceful to wake up. I won't be home until later. How about I swing through town and pick us up some dinner? Mexican?"

"That sounds great. I'll text you later if we decide to go shopping."

"Sounds good. Love you."

"Love you, too," I say before the line goes dead. I stare at my phone, wondering if I really should start dress shopping. I mean, it never hurts to just look around, right? Besides, maybe Jamie needs a dress before next weekend. That's how I can pass it off.

Plan in place, I dial her number. She picks up on the first ring.

"Hey, girl."

"What are you doing today?"

"Not much. Mike is at the bar. I thought about going to see if he needs any help, but you know how he gets when he's in the zone with the books." She laughs.

"That I do. So, about this wedding in two weeks. Do you have a dress?"

"No, I was actually going to just try to find a nice white or off-white sundress or something."

"What do you say we start looking today? Dave is working. I guess they're getting a delivery of horses or something, and since he took a couple of days off this week to help me move, he didn't want to turn them down."

"Sure. Let me take Ace outside and then put him in his cage."

"I'll pick you up. I have to take Dixie out, too, so say thirty minutes?"

"Perfect, see you soon."

I rush through taking Dixie out to pee, which she does, though she still isn't used to her leash and tries to wiggle out of it. "Come on, you little wiggle worm." I laugh, picking her up. "I have to go out, but Daddy and I will be home later to love on you," I promise her. I realize I'm talking to this puppy as if she's my kid, but she's just so damn cute I can't seem to help myself.

After getting Dixie settled with more toys than I know she'll play with, a puppy pad, and a bowl of fresh water, I head out to pick up Jamie. When I pull up to their place, she's sitting on the porch swing, waiting for me.

"Hey, you," she says, climbing into the passenger seat. "Can I just tell you I'm really excited about this?" She grins at me.

"Good. I kind of have a confession, as well," I admit as I pull back out on the road.

"Oh, good, it's not just me. Spill." Her eyes are bright with contentment and love, and I couldn't be happier for her and my big brother.

"So, Dave and I have been talking a lot about the future: weddings and stuff."

"That's not a confession. That man has been asking you to marry him for I don't even know how long."

"Yeah, but that's just it. I told him I was ready. After your engagement party, I told him to surprise me."

"*Eeep!*" she cheers, leaning over to give me an awkward hug over the console. "I'm so happy for you," she says.

"Yeah, so he wants me to start looking for a dress. We talked about wedding plans, and we want simple, and the dress will take the longest, so yeah, I'm kinda looking, too."

"You two should get married with us," she says, excited.

"That's your day, and besides, I've always wanted a country wedding. You know that field of wildflowers at Mom and Dad's?" She nods. "That's where we want to do it. Well, I do, and Dave just agrees. He says he doesn't care as long as the end result is me being his wife." I can feel my smile by just repeating his words.

"Sounds like your brother. When I brought up getting married in the Keys, I was half joking, but he ran with it. So here we are, getting married in just two short weeks."

"I'm not surprised. You guys have been through so much to be together. He's a smart man, my brother."

"He is." She smiles. "So, do you know what kind of dress you're looking for?"

"Something simple, yet elegant. It would have to fit an outdoor wedding. What about you?"

"Same, really. I was just going to find a white sundress. I wasn't sure I'd have time, and then there are alterations…."

"True, but there is the off chance that you could find one that fits perfectly."

"Yeah, I'm thinking something flowy for the beach. Just simple."

I pull into the lot of the local dress shop. "This place has a ton to choose from. Maybe we'll both be lucky."

She holds up her hand, crossing her fingers. "Here's to hoping."

Grabbing my phone, I send a quick text to David.

Me: Hey, Jamie and I are dress shopping.

David: Good news, baby. I hope you find your dream dress.

Me: Not likely on day one.

David: I have a good feeling about it.

Surely it's not going to be as easy as walking into the dress shop, and the first one I see is my dream dress. Could it?

Me: We'll see. Love you.

David: Love you, too, Livy.

Jamie is waiting for me when I finally climb out of the car. "You ready for this?"

"I think so. Are you?"

"Yeah, thanks for doing this."

"Umm, I had an ulterior motive," I remind her.

"Regardless. Thank you."

"Come on, let's go find you a wedding dress."

As soon as we enter the shop, we're greeted with "Welcome to Bridal Memories. What can we do for you today?"

"Well." Jamie looks over at me, smiling. "We need wedding dresses."

"Well, my dears, you've come to the right place. Do you know what you're looking for?"

"I'm having a beach wedding in two weeks, so I'm not sure I can make this happen. But I was thinking something flowy," Jamie says.

"We do alterations in-house, so we can definitely make it happen if you find something we have here in the store. If we have to order it, the alterations depend on shipping time, but we can worry about that once you find a dress. And you?" she asks me.

"We're, uh, just starting to plan," I say, which is not a complete lie. "We're having a small, intimate country wedding outdoors. I want something simple, elegant, but that won't look too out of place in the outdoor setting. A field of wildflowers," I add, just in case that's information she needs.

"Excellent. Let's start with you… I'm sorry, your name is?" She looks at Jamie.

"Jamie, and this is Olivia."

"My name is Hazel. It's lovely to meet both of you. Since your wedding is first, let's take you to the simple flowy section, shall we?" she asks, turning to walk away, and we follow her.

"This place is amazing. You have it so organized."

"Thank you. Planning your special day can be stressful enough, so I try to make it fun and relaxing while you find your dream dress." She smiles kindly. "Can I offer either of you a drink? We have a range of soft drinks and water, plus champagne."

"No, thank you," we both say.

"All right, then, I'll leave you ladies to it. I'll just be right over here if you have any questions." She points to a rack of dresses that she's placing price tags on.

"Where do we start?" Jamie asks, her eyes wide.

"Let's just go to the end and start looking through until something catches your eye."

That's what we do. Jamie begins to sort through each dress one by one, and I stand by, giving my thoughts on those she stops on. They're all beautiful, and I still find it surreal that we're doing this.

"Oh." She pulls a dress off the rack. "I like this one," she says softly, almost as if she's talking to herself.

"Let's try it on. I'll go get Hazel."

As if she heard Jamie, Hazel appears. "Need a fitting room yet?" she asks.

"Yes." Jamie holds the dress up to show Hazel.

"That one is perfect for a beach wedding. Let's get it on you and see what you think." She leads us to a back hallway that has little alcoves with couches and mirrors set up. "We like each bride to have her own space," she explains. She must have noticed the awed expression on my face.

"This is perfect." I take a seat on the couch, setting my purse beside me. "Go." I motion with my hands to send Jamie to the fitting room. "I'll be here, waiting," I tell her.

"Olivia," she calls out a few moments later.

"Yeah?" I stand and go to the fitting room door, thinking she might need help with a zipper.

"I love it," she says, her voice cracking.

"Let me see it." Excitement lifts my voice.

The door opens, and I step back to give her space. She walks to the platforms in the middle of the walls of mirrors and takes her spot.

"Jamie," I breathe, because she looks like a princess. The dress is white, with spaghetti straps and a form-fitting bodice that flows out starting at her thighs. It screams beach wedding, and she looks beautiful.

"You think he'll like it?" she asks with tears in her eyes.

"He's going to love it. This is… perfect." Grabbing my phone from my purse, I take a couple of photos, then show her my phone. "I can't believe the first dress you tried on is it, but it's absolutely perfect."

"Beautiful," Hazel tells her. "It appears as though no alterations are needed. Do you want a veil or a hairpiece?" she asks.

"No, I don't think so. With the wind, I was just going to braid my hair." She pulls her long locks up as if putting them in a ponytail. "I really love it, Olivia. Is this real?" she says with a laugh. "Did I really just find my wedding dress that easily?"

I picture her day in my mind. I can see her on the beach, walking toward my brother. "You did, and it's perfect. Mike is going to love it."

"I'll take it," Jamie squeals.

"Excellent!" Hazel turns to me. "Now, I have just the selection for you. Follow me."

I look at Jamie, and she smiles. "Go while I change. Wait! Can you take a picture for me to show my mom and the girls?"

I grab her phone and mine and snap a few pictures, then follow Hazel to the "perfect section for me" and begin to flip through the dresses with shaking hands.

I'm almost to the end of the rack, and my spirits are dropping because I haven't found one single dress that calls out to me. Then I slide yet another to the right, and I see it. Pulling it off the rack, I take in the details.

It's sleeveless with a V-neck. The entire dress is silk with a lace overlay, A-line, simple yet elegant. Checking the size, I see it's mine, and I slowly make my way toward the fitting room. Jamie and Hazel are zipping her dress into a garment bag.

"Hey, you found one." Jamie looks at the dress in my hands.

"You can use the same room," Hazel says. I nod and disappear behind the door.

I quickly strip out of my clothes and step into the dress. The back is low, so I'm able to reach behind me and zip it up. I stare at my reflection in the mirror, and tears sting my eyes. It's perfect. Exactly what I want.

Grabbing my phone, I pull up David's name and hit the Call button.

"Hey, baby. How's shopping?"

"I found it," I say, my voice cracking. "I found my dress." My hands are shaking. *I can't believe it. The first one.*

"Send me a picture," he says immediately.

"What?" I laugh. "I can't do that. It's bad luck." Though I really do want to show him.

"Come on," he prompts me.

"No." I wipe tears from my cheeks.

"You okay?" he asks.

"Yeah, I just… this is really happening. And Jamie found hers, too. I hope my mom's not upset that she's not here. This is the first one I tried on, and it's perfect, and I have to get it," I ramble on through my tears.

"Of course, you do. She'll understand. It's your dream dress."

"Yeah," I agree.

"Love you, Livy. Buy the dress. I don't care what it costs. But if it brings you to tears, I'm certain you wearing it will bring me to my knees. It's the one," he assures me.

"Okay. I love you, too." I stare at my reflection in the mirror. This is my wedding dress. I do a little wiggle dance as my excitement grows.

"Olivia, let me see," Jamie calls for me.

"I have to go. I'll be home soon," I say and end the call. I'm not even sure if he said goodbye.

I'm standing here in my wedding dress.

This is really happening.

When I open the door, Jamie gasps. "That's it," she says. "How is it possible that we both chose the first dress we tried on?"

"How do you know I'm going to get it?"

"You called him." She points to my phone that's still clutched in my hand. "I called Mike, too." She smiles. "You're getting it. It's perfect. Exactly as you described, simple and elegant."

"Very beautiful," Hazel agrees. "Most go back to the first dress they try on, not trusting their gut with just trying one. You two know what you want. That's a good thing." She walks around me. "Looks like no alterations are needed here either."

"I'll take it."

"Veil? she asks.

I nod. She leads me to the veils, and with Jamie's help, we find one that falls to my waist with the same lace design as the dress. We pay for our dresses, putting dents in our credit cards, and carry them out to my car.

"How about you take mine, and I'll take yours?" Jamie suggests. "Can you bring mine with you to the Keys?"

"Yes." And just like that, we have wedding dresses and a plan to hide them from our fiancés… well, hers and my future.

I still feel weird, but it's happening for us. I just need to be patient.

10

David

Sitting on the beach, watching Mike and Jamie say their vows, sends excitement coursing through me. I'm getting married to the beautiful girl sitting next to me, her head resting on my shoulder as she watches her big brother and one of her closest friends pledge their lives together. The urge is strong to ask her if she wants to do it while we're here. I can call my parents and get them on the next flight out, but I don't. I know it's not what she really wants, and I want to make it the day she's always dreamed of.

I finally know how I'm going to ask her. It's risky as hell, but if I know Olivia, she'll appreciate it. At least, I hope she will. I'm working on finalizing my plans. It's so damn hard not to just go ahead and ask her, but it's going to be worth the wait. I know she's getting worried, but I've tried to assure her as much as I can that we are getting married; she's my forever.

"I can't wait for this day to be ours," she says, snuggling against my chest.

I place my arm around her and kiss the top of her head. Mike and Jamie kiss just as I whisper, "You're going to be a beautiful bride." Green eyes full of love stare up at me.

"Now we toast," Mike announces.

The guest list is simple, just me and Olivia, their parents, and Jamie's parents. That's it. Short, sweet, and simple, and I've never seen two people happier—well, unless you count Olivia and me. I can only hope her smile is as blinding on our wedding day.

Standing, we follow the happy couple and their parents into the private dining room they reserved at the hotel for their mini reception. I thought they would have another when we get home since everyone couldn't make the trip, but they're not. They just want to be married and start the rest of their lives together; that's what Mike told me just before the ceremony. Not that I can blame him. It's what I want, too. I just want her to be my wife. The rest is fluff, details, and none of it holds a candle to my devotion to her.

Dinner is served, and it's just like any other day, two families blended together, now for life. I know better, though. I see the glint in my friend's eyes when he looks at his wife. Not to mention, he's referred to her as his wife at least fifteen times in the last hour. The road they took to get here was winding, but they conquered it. I'm happy for both of them.

"I'm stuffed," Liv says, pushing her plate away from her.

Her plate is half-empty while mine is empty. "Me, too," I agree.

"Time for the first dance." Jamie's mom smiles at her daughter and new son-in-law.

Olivia leans into me, once again resting her head on my shoulder as we watch the happy couple spin around the room, kissing and smiling at one another. I hear a sniff and look down to see her wiping her eyes.

"You okay?"

"Yeah," she says with a chuckle. "I'm just so happy for them. Weddings make me cry anyway, but this is my big brother, and Jamie is one of my closest friends. My heart is just full for them."

"Dance with me," I ask as the song changes.

"There's not really a dance floor," she reminds me, scanning the room.

"Don't care." I stand and offer her my hand, and she takes it. I guide her over to the side of the room, where Mike and Jamie are still wrapped in each other's arms, as if the change in song didn't even register to them.

Jamie spots us and smiles. "You two are next," she tells us.

"We are," I agree. I've never made it a secret that I want to spend the rest of my life with Olivia. Hell, I talked to her parents months ago. Everyone knows, and I'm good with that. I want to shout it from the rooftops, letting the world know that the beautiful woman in my arms is going to be my wife.

I pull Liv a little closer as we sway to the beat of the song. My hand lazily strokes up and down her back, and I love the feel of her in my arms.

"I can't wait to be your wife." Her whispered confession travels straight to my dick.

"Now look what you did," I say, pulling her even closer so my hard length is pressed into her.

"Really?"

"Yep. Just thinking about you being my wife, every damn time. This time you said it, so yeah—"

"I feel terrible." She pretends to be sad, but I can read right through her. "Maybe we should go back to the room, you know, because you're not feeling well." She wiggles her hips just slightly, rubbing against me. "I'm sure it's… painful."

"Thank you all for being here," Mike says, pulling us out of our lust-filled conversation. He looks down at Jamie. "My wife and I just wanted to start our lives together. And to have you here to be a part of that is something we'll never forget." Jamie goes up on her tiptoes and kisses him. "Now, if you'll excuse us, we have a villa to get to."

We all laugh, knowing it's not the villa they're rushing off for. With a round of hugs and congratulations, they're off, and the rest of us say goodbye and head to our respective rooms.

"Remind me to thank your brother," I say as we step onto the elevator to head to our room.

"Why's that?"

"I was about to pull you from that room, and there would have been no doubt as to why."

As if she needs a reminder, I reach down and adjust my dick that's pressing against my zipper. When the elevator doors open, I place my hand on the small of her back and lead us to our room. Reaching into my wallet, I pull out our room card and insert it into the lock. The lock releases, and Olivia turns the handle, walking into the room with me on her heels.

I drop my wallet and the key card onto the dresser, pulling my phone and hers from my pocket and setting them on the table, as well. She's facing away from me, sitting on the edge of the bed, unstrapping her heels. One by one, I open the buttons on my shirt before sliding my arms out of the sleeves and tossing it across the chair. Next come my shorts and underwear, which also get tossed on the chair. Taking my hard cock in my hand, I stroke from root to tip, watching her. When she stands and turns to face me, mouth open, probably to ask what I want to do the rest of the night, she pauses. She closes her mouth, her eyes going to my hand and cock.

"You started without me," she breathes.

"You'd better catch up, then." I watch her, my eyes following her hands as she slips out of her yellow sundress, letting it fall to the floor. She's wearing a pale-yellow bra and matching panties, which stand out like a beacon against her bronzed skin. Reaching behind her back, she unclasps her bra and slowly, torturously so, slides one strap and then the other over her slender shoulders before letting it fall to the floor.

Her breasts are firm and round, begging for my mouth. I want to rush to her, pull her naked body against mine, and devour her. Trace every inch of her soft skin with my tongue, show her with my body what she means to me. Instead, I hold steady, stroking my cock. "Keep going," I urge her. She needs to lose the panties. If I get any closer, I'll end up ripping them off her.

"Like this?" she asks coyly. I watch as her fingers wrap around the slender band of her lace panties. She pulls them over her hips and down her legs, kicking them to the side.

"Better," I say, taking her in. "You're beautiful, Livy." I take a step toward her. One foot after the other, I move until my arms wrap around her waist and tug her against me. This right here, her in my arms, makes everything right in my world.

"Make love to me." She looks up at me, those green eyes showing me that the love that's pulsing through my veins is in hers, as well.

Placing my lips over hers, I kiss her. The taste of her on my tongue only fuels my desire. Hands on her thighs, I pick her up and carry her to the bed. Climbing onto it with her tiny frame still wrapped around me, I settle her head on the pillow. After breaking the kiss, I trail my lips across her jaw and down her slender neck.

"Dave," she whispers.

I lift my head, my eyes meeting hers. What I see is my undoing. So much love, want, need—all for me. Dropping my head to her chest, I suck a pert nipple into my mouth, loving it with my tongue. Her back arches off the bed, silently asking for more. Not one to disappoint my girl, I release her hard nipple with a pop and trail kisses to the other, giving it the same attention.

"Please," she hums. Her eyes are closed, her back still arched, head tilted to the side as she waits for me to give her what she wants.

I don't move, waiting for her to open her eyes. I want her to be looking at me when I slide deep inside of her.

"There she is," I whisper against her lips when her eyes open and watch me. "I love you, Livy," I say, pushing inside of her.

"Love you," she replies, digging her nails into my back.

I take just a minute to cherish the feeling of being home, because that's what it is. Every time I'm inside of her, a sense of belonging washes over me, like this is where I'm meant to be.

The urge to ask her to marry me is strong. The words are on the tip of my tongue, but I know this isn't how I want to do it. Not to mention, I don't have her ring. But I crave the sound of her saying yes. Instead, I press my lips to hers to keep me from shouting the words and rock my hips.

"R-right th-there," she stammers, locking her legs around my hips, drawing her closer. Deeper.

"Baby, I'm close," I warn.

"Mmm," she moans and then cries out my name.

With my hands braced beside her head against the mattress, I withdraw and thrust back inside. Her walls squeeze me like a vise as I call out her name and fall over the edge.

Resting my forehead against hers, I try to catch my breath. Every time with her feels like the first time. The way her body wraps around mine, as if she were made for me, it's perfect. She's perfect for me.

Sliding out of her, I roll to my side and pull her into my chest.

"I should go clean up," she pants.

"Just lie here like this. Let me hold you, baby."

After a few minutes, her breathing evens out, and I know she's asleep. I can't wait until the day that it's our wedding that we just left, and the first time I get to make love to her as my wife. My cock stirs at the thought, and I have to close my eyes and focus on her even breathing to calm the hell down.

Kissing the top of her head, I whisper the words into the darkness of the room. "Marry me." I know she's asleep, but I need to say what's in my heart, and those two words, they say so much.

11

Olivia

Placing the finishing touches on the gift for Whitney and Aaron's baby shower, I set it on the counter and clean up my mess from the wrapping paper. I might have gone a little overboard with the clothes, but they're too cute not to. The gift bag is full of individually wrapped presents.

"Guys go to these things?" David asks as he enters the room, pulling his black T-shirt over his head.

"Yeah, some do. Depends on the couple. Aaron is really involved, so it's a co-ed shower." Not that it would matter. David is the kind of man who, if I asked him to be there, he would be there.

He comes up behind me and wraps his arms around my waist, placing a soft kiss on my neck. "Is that how we're going to do it?" he whispers.

"Is that how you want it?"

Sliding his large, calloused hand under my shirt, he rests his palm just above my belly button. "I don't want to miss a single second, so yeah, that's how I want it. You good with that?"

I turn in his arms, my hands snaking up around his neck. "I

wouldn't want it any other way." On tiptoes, I press my lips to his—just a peck, but that doesn't matter. Any time my mouth is pressed to his, any time he's near, my body heats. My desire for him is that strong.

"You about ready to go?" he asks.

"Yeah, I'm finished with the gifts. I just need to grab my purse and phone."

"I'll take this." He steps back, releasing his hold on me, and grabs the bag from the counter. "Sheesh," he says, acting as if the bag is too heavy for him.

"Ha-ha," I say dryly. "I can't help it." I stick my tongue out at him.

"You're amazing." He kisses the corner of my mouth. "I'll take this out to the truck."

"Thank you. I'll be right there." I grab my purse and phone and lock the door behind me.

Aaron greets us as soon as we walk through the door. "Glad you could make it," he says, kissing me on the cheek and shaking David's hand.

"Where do we put this?" David holds up the gift bag in his hands.

"This way. Olivia, Whit's in the dining room with her feet up. At least, they better be. McKinley's better be, too. Jamie's in there, enforcing the rule. Well, all the women are, actually, except for our mom and my aunts, who are fussing over the food."

"Thanks." David gives my hip a gentle squeeze before following Aaron to the gift table.

"We were wondering when you were going to get here," Jamie teases as I enter the dining room.

"I found a couple more last-minute gifts that I had to wrap." I look over at Whit, who has her feet propped up on a chair, just as her husband had said she was supposed to be doing. "How you feeling?"

"Hard to maneuver." She smiles, rubbing her beach ball of a belly.

"Well, you look beautiful. How was your doctor's appointment?"

Her eyes light up. "Good, good," she says, and I feel as though she's leaving something out. I raise my eyebrows, and she just smiles at me. No doubt she'll tell us when she's ready.

"I was showing them the pictures from the wedding," Jamie says, passing me the photo album.

"When did they come in?" I ask her.

"Today. We were pulling out when the mail lady stopped at the box. I refused to leave until she was gone so I could check the mail." She laughs.

"I don't blame you." I open the album and skim through the pictures. "Wow, these are gorgeous. That photographer got some great shots."

"He really did. Thank you for finding him."

"I didn't, not really. I called the hotel and asked for recommendations. He was highly acclaimed. We got lucky that there was a last-minute booking that canceled. I didn't ask it if was a wedding because I didn't want to know. Feels wrong to be so happy when someone may not be."

"I can see why," McKinley agrees. "As for the other couple, you just have to worry about you. Maybe they eloped, or she went into labor?" she offers.

"You ladies ready?" Aaron asks, joining us. "Everyone's here." He smiles at his wife, bending down to run his hand over her baby bump.

Evan comes in with Walker on his hip, offering McKinley his hand. She's due any day now with baby number three. "You feeling okay?" he asks her.

I watch as she smiles up at him. "I'm fine, Evan. Where's Lex?"

"She's telling Mike and David about her new horse, even though they've both already seen him," he says with a laugh.

Jamie and I stand and follow them to the main living room, where the gifts are set up and folding chairs have been added. I take a seat next to David, and he slips his arm around my shoulders, keeping his eyes trained on Lex as she tells him about how pretty her new horse is.

"Thanks for coming, everyone," Aaron says. "Sorry it's such a tight space, but it's easier on my wife being here than having to pack everything home. Before we get started, we wanted to make an announcement." He looks down at Whitney with love shining in his eyes. "Whit and I had a doctor's appointment yesterday, and well, we're having twins!" he says excitedly.

"How long have you known?" Aaron's mom asks, wiping tears from her face.

"A while, but we wanted to wait until today and surprise everyone."

"I'm as big as a house. McKinley is due any day now, and I'm bigger than she is," Whitney jokes. "I don't think it was a very well-kept secret. You wondered, right?" She looks at Jamie and me, and we nod. None of us is willing to say out loud that she was already bigger than she would be with a single baby.

"The thought did cross my mind," Aaron's mom confesses. "But I thought for sure you would have told us." She pauses. "Twins." She stands from her chair and embraces her son and daughter-in-law.

Once congratulations and hugs are passed around, we start the games. "How in the hell am I supposed to guess the candy bar?" David asks. "And this is just… gross. Seriously, this is what y'all do at baby showers?"

I throw my head back in laughter. "It's baby themed."

"Well, we're not playing this game at our shower," he grumbles.

"Really? I would have thought you would want to see Aaron suffer."

"Maybe," he says, not really committing as he passes a newborn diaper full of what I think is a Snickers bar over to Mike and Jamie.

The next game we play is the toilet paper game, where we have to guess how much toilet paper will fit around Whitney's belly. David, Mike, and Evan all bowed out, saying there is no winner when you have to guess "how big" a woman is. After a word search, we went to the gifts. I volunteered to write down each item and from whom, so they could write their thank-you notes later.

"Do you have one of these for every kid?" Mike asks.

"No, just the first one. Although, if there's a lot of time between babies, some have another."

"Too many rules," Dave grumbles beside me. "I say have one for each kid. It's a celebration, right? And from the looks of all this loot, kids need a lot," he says, looking around the room.

"Well, in this case it's two babies at once, so all this" —I point to the gift bags, baskets, and piles of gifts—"is going to come in handy for sure."

"Def—" McKinley starts but stops, placing her hand on her back.

"You okay?" Evan asks her.

"Y-yeah. But I think we need to go to the hospital," she says, calm as ever.

"Is it the baby? What's wrong?" I ask.

She looks up at me, her face pained. "Yeah, my water just broke."

"What?" This has Whitney climbing to her feet with Aaron's assistance. "You're in labor? Are you okay? What can we do?"

"Yes, and my water broke." She looks down at her lap and back up at her brother and his wife. "Sorry."

"Nothing to be sorry for," Whit assures her.

"I'll take the kids. Go, have your baby. We'll bring Lex and Walker over once he's here," I say, rubbing her shoulder, trying to soothe her in some way.

"We'll drive," Mike offers, ushering Jamie out of the house to help her into the truck.

"You sure you don't mind keeping the kids? I don't want Mom to have to deal with them and the shower," McKinley explains.

"We got it," David assures her.

"Thank you," Evan says. Then he yells out for Lexi.

"Hi, Daddy," she says, hugging his knees.

"Hey, sweetie, Mommy and I need to go to the hospital. Your baby brother is being born. Can you be a big girl and help Olivia and David take care of Walker while we're gone? I'll call them as soon as he's here and have them bring you to the hospital."

Lexi nods, her little head bobbing up and down. She studies McKinley, who's struggling through another contraction. "Don't worry, Mommy. Daddy will take care of you. He's really good at it."

"I know, sweet girl. You be good for Olivia and David, and take good care of Walker for us."

"I will, Mommy." She skips off, yelling for her little brother, who isn't old enough to understand what's going on, but she's telling him anyway.

"Thank you," Evan says again as he helps McKinley stand. He and her mother walk her out to the truck, where Mike and Jamie are waiting to take them to the hospital.

12

David

Instead of going back to our place, we got a spare key from McKinley's mom and took the kids to their house. Lexi and Olivia are playing dress-up—well, Lex is. Olivia is letting her fix her hair. Me, I'm just hanging out on the couch with my man Walker. He fell asleep on the way here, and when I tried to lay him down when we got into the house, he started to cry. I picked him back up, and he fell right back asleep, so I'm lounging on the couch, with him sleeping on my chest, watching my girl and Lexi.

"It's so pretty, Aunt Livy," Lexi tells her.

I'm an only child, so being an uncle will come only from my wife's family. That means that Mike and Jamie need to get busy. Not that I don't claim Lexi and Walker, because I do, but I'm more of a stand-in uncle. With Mike and Jamie's kids, it'll be the real thing. I can't wait to be an uncle, and if I'm honest, a father. I've imagined Olivia pregnant several times, and it does the same thing to me as thinking about her being my wife does. I'd be concerned that I'm some kind of creep, but it only happens with Olivia. I've come to the conclusion that it's okay, not creepy at all, since that woman owns my heart and soul.

Walker whimpers, turning his head to look the other way. Lexi jumps to her feet and runs her little hands up and down his back. "This is what Mommy and Daddy do when he cries." She climbs up on the couch, rests her head on my shoulder, and continues to rub her little brother's back, soothing him.

"You're a great big sister, Lexi," I tell her.

"That's what my daddy says," she says, yawning.

"Hey, Lex, I have an idea. Why don't we watch a movie?"

"Okay," she agrees, not bothering to move.

"What should we watch?" Olivia asks her.

"Walker likes *Cars*. Tow Mater is his favorite."

"He's sleeping. We can watch your favorite," I tell her.

"I like it, too, and that way, if hims wakes up, he can watch it, too."

This little person, she's awesome. I hope our kids are half as cool as she is. I catch my future wife's eyes, and she smiles. Olivia makes quick work of putting in the DVD and settles on the other side of Lex on the couch.

"You wanna snuggle with me?" Olivia asks Lexi.

Lexi simply reaches out and pulls Olivia next to her, so the four of us are close together. It's not a bad way to spend the afternoon, that's for sure.

I'm just about to sleep when I hear Olivia's phone alert with a text message. I watch as she pulls it out of her pocket, carefully, so as not to disturb Lexi, who has fallen asleep against my arm, just like her little brother.

I watch as she reads the message, then turns to me and smiles. "Healthy baby boy," she whispers. She holds up her phone so I can see, and on the screen is a tiny little baby, with a red, scrunched-up face, swaddled in a blanket. "They named him Beau," she whispers.

"Everyone doing well?" I whisper back.

She nods, tears in her eyes. "Yeah, all is well. They said we can take the kids whenever we're ready," she says, not taking her eyes off the screen. "I told them we would once they wake up from their nap, and we'll get them something to eat." She turns to look at me. "I hope that's okay.

"Of course, it is. These little people need to meet their new baby brother." As soon as I say that, Lexi sits up and looks around. I'm sure she's wondering why she's waking up beside me and not her dad.

"Do I have another brother?" she asks groggily.

Olivia pulls her into her lap and snuggles her. "Yes, you do. His name is Beau, and as soon as Walker wakes up, we're going to get some food in your tummy and then go meet him."

Walker stirs, and Lexi cheers, causing him to jump and lift his head from my shoulder. He looks at me, then his sister and Olivia, then back at me. His bottom lip juts out, and I know I have mere seconds before this little guy starts to cry. Quickly, I stand from the couch and run my hand up and down his back just like Lexi did.

"It's okay, little man," I tell him. "Are you hungry?"

"Hims likes McDonald's," Lexi informs us.

I throw my head back in laughter, which causes Walker to grin. "McDonald's, huh? What does he get?"

"A happy meal," she says, like I should have already known this information. "But hims get plain burgers 'cause they are so messy. You hafta help him with it, 'cause hims so little. I get nuggets."

"That solves that." Olivia grins. "Let's take you to the potty and change Walker's diaper, and we'll go to McDonald's."

"Yay!" Lex jumps off the couch and races down the hall.

Olivia takes Walker from me.

"You need help?"

"No, I got it. We'll be ready to go in ten. Maybe grab the diaper bag. We don't want to walk out and forget that."

"Got it." I kiss her, which has Walker pushing me away again, making me laugh. "I get it, buddy. I want her all to myself, too."

My girl smiles and rolls her eyes, then disappears down the hall.

My phone rings. Pulling it out, I see it's Aaron. "Hey, man."

"Hey, did you hear? Baby boy."

"We did. We're taking the kids to get something to eat, then running them by the hospital to meet him."

"That's why I'm calling. We're done here. Whit and I are going to keep the kids at our place tonight."

"You sure? We can help."

"Yeah, thanks, man. We're heading to the hospital, too, so we'll wait on y'all and take the kids home with us."

"Sounds like a plan. We need to bring anything from the house?" I ask him, looking around.

"Just the diaper bag. They both have clothes and toys here."

"Got it. See you soon." Sliding my phone back into my pocket, I go in search of the diaper bag. Opening it up, I see there are four diapers. I don't know much about babies—well, he's a toddler now—but I'm guessing four is not going to be enough. Grabbing the bag, I head to his room, where Olivia is just slipping his shorts back over his legs. I tell her about the call with Aaron, and she points to the huge stack of diapers underneath the table Walker is lying on. I grab two handfuls and place them in the bag. Never can be too prepared, at least that's my thought.

"You have enough there?" Olivia laughs.

"Hey, this is important stuff," I tell her. "When we have kids, we're just going to keep a pack of these in our cars. Just in case."

Her laugh grows louder. "That's not necessary."

I point to my chest. "Boy Scout."

"What's so funny?" Lex asks from the doorway.

"Nothing, sweetie. You're going to spend the night with Uncle Aaron and Aunt Whitney. Is there anything you want to take with you?"

"Yay!" She runs off to her room and comes back with a small purple blanket. "That one." She points toward the crib, where a blue one just like it sits crumpled on the mattress. "He sleeps with his, too."

Walking over, I grab the blanket, intending to shove it into the diaper bag, as well, but Walker grunts and reaches for it, so I hand it over instead. We get the kids loaded into my truck in their car seats, and I head toward McDonald's. Lexi chatters in the back seat to Walker, and he babbles right back to her, as if they're having a real conversation. Who knows? Maybe they are.

Reaching over the console, I hold my hand open, palm up, and Liv places hers in mine. "This will be our life in a few years," I tell her.

"Yeah? Two by then, you think?" She chuckles.

"Maybe. Who knows. We could have twins, too."

"Hey." She pretends to be offended. "One at a time, mister."

I shrug, not taking my eyes off the road. "Can't help it if my boys are good swimmers."

"I'm a good swimmer," Lexi says from the back seat. "My daddy taught me. Do you have boys, Uncle David? How come I never met them before?" she asks.

I bite my lip to keep from laughing, and Olivia looks horrified. "I was just teasing about my friends." I glance in the rearview mirror at Lex.

"Oh, my daddy is your friend, right? And Uncle Aaron and Uncle Mike. I've seen them swim before. They are good swimmers," she informs us.

Chancing a quick look at Olivia, I see her shoulders shaking in silent laughter, as are mine. "From the mouth of babes," I whisper, and she squeezes my hand tightly in hers.

This right here is what I want for us. I can't wait to put my plan in motion.

13

Olivia

I have to admit, girls' nights are not what they used to be. We used to meet up at my family's bar, have a few drinks, and then the guys would drive us home. Once McKinley was pregnant with Walker, we moved them to one of our houses, but there was still alcohol.

"Can I have my turn now?" I'm fully aware that I'm whining, but baby Beau has been snuggled by everyone but me, and my sister-in-law is the current baby hog.

Everyone laughs. "I guess," Jamie says, like I'm a huge inconvenience to her.

"Finally!" I walk to where she's sitting in the recliner and carefully accept baby Beau into my arms. "Look at you," I coo down at him. "You're just the cutest little man." Yeah, I know he doesn't understand me, but I can't resist.

"Y'all need anything from the kitchen?" McKinley asks. She's moving around great for a woman who just gave birth to this little guy a little over three weeks ago.

"Do you mind grabbing me a water?" Whitney asks. She's posted on the love seat, her feet propped up on the table, her hands on her baby belly.

"Olivia, Jamie, either of you ready for that glass of wine?" Her voice is wistful, as if she's living through us. She's nursing, so no alcohol for her. McKinley refuses the pump-and-dump method. She's strict as can be when it comes to her babies. Not that I blame her; I'd be the same way.

"I'm good right now, thanks," I say, not taking my eyes off the sleeping baby in my arms.

"Jamie?" McKinley asks again.

"Uh, just water for me, too."

Her voice is off. I look up and study her; she looks nervous as hell. "What's up with you?" I ask her.

"What? Nothing," she says way too quickly. I hold her stare and see the moment she caves. "I'm pregnant," she says softly.

"I'm going to be an aunt?" I say too loudly, causing little Beau to jump in my arms. "Shh," I soothe him back to sleep. "I'm going to be an aunt?" I say again, softer this time.

"Yeah." She smiles. "You're going to be an aunt."

"How far along are you?" I ask, fighting the tears that are threatening to fall.

"Eight weeks." She blushes. "When we decided to get married in the Keys, I stopped taking my birth control. We didn't want to wait," she tells us.

"I'm so happy for you," I say as I lose the battle with my tears. I look down at Beau and then back to Jamie. "You're going to have one of these," I murmur. "My brother is going to be a daddy." I laugh.

"He is, and he's excited. We were going to wait until the first trimester ended, but I knew I would end up spilling the beans tonight. He told me to go for it."

"Thank you." I look Jamie in the eye. "Thank you for loving him, for bringing him to life and giving our family this gift."

She wipes at her tears. "He's my heart."

"What about you?" Whitney asks. "Any wedding news?"

"No. I mean, he says we're going to be married, and he even suggested I buy a dress, which I did." I blush.

"What? When? We would have gone with you," McKinley says, passing out bottles of water.

"She went with me," Jamie says. "Called me out of the blue, asked if I had a dress, and we went shopping. We both fell in love with the first dresses we tried on, and the rest, as they say, is history," she explains.

"Does he know you found a dress?"

"He does. He keeps trying to get me to show it to him."

"Show it to us," Whitney tells me.

Grabbing my phone from the arm of the couch, I unlock the screen and pass it to McKinley, who *oohs* and *aahs* and then passes it to Whit. "That's beautiful," McKinley says.

"It really is," Whit agrees.

"So, has he asked you?" Jamie chimes in.

"No. He went from asking me at least once a week to radio silence. Well, not really radio silence, but he hasn't asked me once since then. We talked about it. He said he's only getting down on one knee once in his life, and he needs to do it right. Then he said it was happening. We talked about the wedding and what I've always dreamed it would be. He said he doesn't care as long as I'm the one walking down the aisle."

They all melt at that. I can see the soft expressions on their faces, not to mention the rounds of "He's so sweet."

"He said what I want is simple, and it sounded to him like the dress is the hardest part, so he told me to start looking. I never dreamed I would find the dress day one, let alone the first one I tried on. I bought it and sent it home with Jamie."

"He loves you," Jamie assures me. "You can't look at that man when you're around and not see it."

"She's right," McKinley agrees. "He's always looked at you like that."

"He's planning the grand gesture, I'm sure of it. It's obvious he's no longer playfully asking you because the next time he does, he's going to be on one knee, and you'd better say yes." She points at me.

I can't help but laugh at her. "I'm so saying yes. I know you guys are right, but I'm anxious for it to happen. I spent all this time letting worry keep us from moving forward, and now that I'm ready, I feel like we're at a standstill."

"I get that," McKinley says. "But you have to understand, he's wanted you to be his wife for almost as long as y'all have been together. He's not a man to half-ass his once-in-a-lifetime proposal."

"I agree," Jamie adds. "He wants it to be perfect. It's happening. He's not stringing you along. He's not like that."

"I know that, in reality, but I can't help but be mad at myself for keeping us from this for months."

"You weren't ready," Whitney reassures me. "He knew that, and so did you. Now you are, and it'll happen. Have a little faith."

"I want babies. Y'all are so far ahead of me," I say, wiping a tear from my eyes.

"Not really. I have two more months," Whit explains.

"And I have seven," Jamie adds. "Regardless, we're going to be raising our kids together. I'm not stopping at one." She laughs. "At least, I hope not. So what, our kids aren't the exact same age? They're still going to grow up as family. All of them." She looks around the room.

"I know, I just—"

"You're just impatient." McKinley laughs. "You always have been."

"It's hard not to be when I'm holding this little guy, or when he talks about our future."

"He's always done that," Whitney says gently. "He waited a long time for you to tell him that you were ready to move forward. Give him this time to make it special for you. You said he told you he didn't care how big or small the wedding was, just that he wanted you to be the one walking down the aisle toward him. Maybe the proposal is what he cares about. Maybe he wants a story to tell your kids and grandkids. Maybe he wants to blow your romantic fantasies out of the water."

"Y'all are Team David tonight," I laugh.

"No, we're Team Olivia and David," Jamie says. "We want you both to be happy. We can see it from the outside looking in. It's going to happen."

"I know. He loves me. I'm so damn lucky to have him in my life. I just… want it all. Now," I admit with a laugh.

"See, impatient." McKinley nods.

"Fine, I'm impatient," I agree. At the risk of sounding like a broken record, I continue. "I know I'm the one who kept us from moving forward, and well, I just thought that the night I told him I was ready, it would be soon."

Before the girls can reply, the front door opens, and Evan, followed by Aaron, Mike, and my man, walk into the room. I watch as each of them makes a beeline for their girl.

"Livy," David says, taking a seat next to me. "Have a good night?"

"We did. How about you?"

"Played a few games of pool over at Aaron's." He places a kiss just beneath my ear. "Missed you," he whispers.

I turn to look at him, a smile on my face.

"That's what I want," he says softly, just low enough for me to hear. "I want that smile on your face every day for the rest of our lives."

I don't have words, so I lean in and press my lips to his. My love for this man grows every damn day. I never want to know what it's like to not have him in my life.

14

David

"Where are you taking me?" Liv asks from the seat beside me.

We're in my truck, headed to our date. "If I tell you, that will ruin the surprise."

"I love your surprises, but I also love knowing." She laughs.

"How was your day?" I rushed home from work, grabbed a shower, and we raced out the door. She's known about this date all week, so she was ready when I got home.

"Good. We interviewed a new bartender to rotate and give the others some weekend nights off. Mike and I both liked her."

"Good. You offer the job?"

"Not yet. We're waiting for her references to come back, but I have a good feeling about her. My gut tells me she's going to be a great part of the team."

"That's great. Y'all need that. I'm sure the others will appreciate it, too."

"Yeah, I mean, you have to enjoy your job, and no one likes working every single weekend night. This way, we can keep our good bartenders, add another good one to the roster, I hope, and keep everyone happy."

"I'm proud of you," I tell her. "You're stepping up instead of hiding in the shadows, and look at what you're doing, helping make Mike's Tavern even better. I know Mike appreciates it."

"Does he? I mean, he tells me, but it's nice to know he also told you." She smiles over at me.

"Yeah, especially with Jamie and now the baby. He likes the fact that the two of you share the burden, but neither of you has to live there. It's a well-oiled machine the two of you are running. You should both be proud."

"I am." Her voice is soft. "I don't know where the idea that my kids would be embarrassed, or even you would, came from by me working there, but I really do love it. I love it even more that I'm not there every night, and I get to come home to you at the end of the day."

I don't answer right away; instead, I wait until I reach the stop sign. Checking there's no one behind me, I reach over the console and slide my hand behind her neck, pulling her lips to mine. I kiss her, tracing her lips with my tongue. "That's my favorite," I tell her. "Nothing is better than coming home to you and waking up with you in our home. We're living the dream, Livy." I rest my forehead against hers. "I love you, Olivia." Before she can answer, a horn sounds from behind us.

Her laughter fills the truck as I pull away from her, check both ways, and drive through the stop sign. "Love you, too," she tells me through her laughter.

That sound, that smile, it's my addiction. I just hope tonight ends with that same sound falling from her lips and that smile gracing her beautiful face. I'm nervous as we get closer to our destination, which I know is ridiculous, but it's the truth all the same. I want to wipe my sweaty palms on my jeans, but that would give me away; instead, I keep both hands on the wheel. I want to reach over and lace her fingers with mine, but I refrain, keeping both hands on the wheel and driving as if my insides are not twisted.

"Where are we going?" she asks again. I've just turned on the road to her parents' house. "Are we going to Mom and Dad's?"

"We are," I confess.

"We're having date night with my parents?"

"Not exactly."

"I'm totally confused."

"Just be patient."

"This is me you're talking to."

I laugh. "I know, baby, but you'll find out what I have planned soon. I promise."

We pull into her parents' drive, and all the lights are off. Just like we planned, they left the house tonight to give us this time together. "Looks like they're not even home," she says, looking at the same dark house.

"Nope. They went out to dinner."

"Do you have some fantasy of us getting a little freaky in my childhood bedroom or something?" She's half joking, half serious by the tone of her voice.

"No." I laugh. "Although, now that you mention it…" She reaches over and lightly smacks my arm, causing me to laugh even harder. Driving past the house, I park my truck by the old barn. "Stay here. I'll be right back." Rushing out of the truck, I make my way inside the barn and fire up the Gator. The bed is already packed with a picnic basket, blanket, and champagne, everything we'll need for our night together. I even grabbed a hoodie for both of us, just in case it gets too chilly. Eventually, she'll find out that I wasn't at work today; I was here, making this night special for her. At least, I hope it is.

I drive the Gator up to her side of the truck and hop off, making my way to her door as she pushes her door open. "What are you doing?"

"Come with me." I offer her my hand, and she takes it, jumping out of the truck. I guide her to the passenger side of the Gator, and she climbs on.

"I told you it's a surprise," I say when I see she's about to ask me again. "Just be patient with me." I kiss her lips lightly before rushing around and getting behind the wheel of the Gator. We drive in silence, me because I have a million different scenarios running through my mind, though her, I'm not sure. A quick glance tells me she's enjoying the scenery. It's just about sunset, and I know she loves this time of day.

"Are we going to the field of wildflowers?"

"We are," I concede.

"I haven't been here at sunset in years. This is a great idea," she assures me. She glances back at the bed of the Gator and sees the blanket and picnic basket. "You're pulling out all the stops," she teases.

"Nothing but the best for my girl."

We reach the front edge of the field, and I stop. Just over the knoll is yet another surprise for her, but I need to take this one step at a time. "This looks like a good spot."

"It's perfect," she agrees.

So far, so good. "Give me a minute to get everything set up."

"I can help."

"Just sit tight." I kiss her lips, just a quick peck before getting to work setting up our spot for the night. I spread out a king-size quilt, which gives us plenty of room, keeping the extra blanket folded in one corner with our sweatshirts on top of it. Then I unpack the picnic basket, setting it off to the side, as well. I stopped by earlier today and mowed this area, just outside of the wildflowers, for this very reason. I'm surprised she hasn't commented on the fact. Hopefully, she's too busy with the view to notice, at least not yet. I need to get through my surprise for her first. Both of them.

Once everything is set up, I go to her side of the Gator and offer my hand. "Ready?"

She smiles up at me and nods. As soon as she climbs out, I bend down and pick her up bridal-style, carrying her to the blanket.

"I can walk," she tells me, but her smile tells me more. She likes this, and that helps to relieve my nerves just a little. Setting her feet on the blanket, I cup her face in my hands and kiss her. I try to show her with the gentle glide of my tongue against hers everything I'm about to say, or at least, I hope to. I've practiced this a million and one times. I just hope I don't fuck it up, as nervous as I am.

"I know you can," I say, breaking our kiss. "However, I like you in my arms better."

"It is a nice place to be."

"Let's sit," I suggest, and she drops to her knees.

"What is all of this?"

"Well, we have chicken salad sandwiches, Cool Ranch Doritos, and peanut butter pie for dessert. Water to drink." I keep the bottle of champagne in the basket with the two fancy plastic flutes I picked up a week ago.

"All my favorites. Are you trying to get lucky?"

"I'm hoping that if I play my cards right, tonight will most certainly be my lucky night." I lean in and kiss her again, just because I want to, just because I can. It might also be so I don't blurt the words out right here, right now. I was expecting to see a gleam in her eyes, one that tells me that she knows what I'm up to, but so far, if she does know, she hasn't let on. Then again, maybe I'm just too damn nervous to pick up on it.

We eat our dinner, talking about anything and everything. That's how it is with us; it's always been so damn easy. Loving her is easy.

"What are your plans this weekend?" I ask her.

"I've got nothing, unless you do. I texted the girls earlier this week, asking if they needed anything with the new babies and pregnancies, but they assured me they're all good. They plan on just having a quiet weekend in, so I figured maybe we could do the same."

"Any time with you is time well spent." Packing up our leftovers in the picnic basket, I lean back and open my legs, patting the spot between them. "Come here." She doesn't hesitate to crawl over to me, her back against my chest. I wrap my arms around her as we watch the sunset over the trees.

"I really love this place," she says softly.

"It's beautiful."

"I hope my parents never sell. If they do, do you think we could consider buying it?"

"Babe, you have nothing to worry about. This is their home and will be for years to come. You'll be able to bring our kids here."

"Yeah, and I can tell them how their dad made me a romantic picnic dinner in my favorite spot, and we watched the sunset together."

"I don't know. If this is a story for our kids one day, I need to step up my game." I nuzzle her neck before whispering in her ear, "Stand up."

She doesn't even question me, just climbs to her feet. I follow after her, pulling my phone out of my pocket and turning on some music. Brantley Gilbert's "Fall into Me" croons from my phone's speaker as I toss it to the blanket and pull her into my arms. I hold her tightly as we barely sway to the music.

Just as the song ends, I pull back and drop to my knees. I can see the confusion on her face, then clarity as I reach into my pocket and pull out a ring. Not just any ring, her ring, the one I hope she agrees to wear for the rest of her life.

"Olivia," I say, my voice cracking. I swallow hard. "I've loved you for longer than I can remember. I want to grow old with you. I want to sit on the back porch and watch our kids and our grandkids grow. I want to hold you when times are tough and laugh with you when they're not. I want your name attached to mine. I want you to fall into me." A tear slides down her cheek, and I ache to brush it away with my thumb, but I have yet to ask her that one important question. "Livy, will you do me the incredible honor of becoming my wife? Will you marry me?"

She's nodding before I even have the question out. "Yes," she murmurs through her tears. "A thousand times yes." She drops to her knees and crushes her mouth against mine.

"Baby, as much as I love this," I say against her lips, "can I give you your ring?"

She laughs, a beautiful sound that soothes my soul. "I love you." She kisses me one more time, then pulls away and holds out her hand.

I slide the round diamond solitaire, surrounded by smaller round diamonds with rows of them on the band as well, onto her finger, and I swear, her smile sparkles just as much as the ring.

"Good surprise?" I ask her.

"The best." She wraps her arms around me in a hug, and I gently fall back on the blanket, bringing her with me. We get lost in each other, kissing like teenagers, neither one of us willing to or wanting to break our connection. We kiss until the sun has finally set beyond the trees, the stars and the moon our only light.

When we finally come up for air, she rests her head on my chest, and I hold her tightly. This moment is one I will never forget in my lifetime. Every detail will forever be etched into my memory.

"This was perfect," she whispers. "Definitely a story to tell our kids one day."

"You think so?" I ask her.

"Most definitely."

"I don't know, I was kinda thinking I still need to step up my game a little."

"You can't be serious." She raises her head to look at me. "This was the most romantic proposal ever. In my favorite spot with my favorite person. What more could a girl ask for?"

Here goes nothing. "Well, I have one more surprise for you."

"What else could there possibly be?" she asks.

I run my fingers through her hair, pushing it back from her eyes. "There's still something," I admit. "However, I'm more nervous about this one than I was to propose."

"You were nervous?"

"Hell yes, I was nervous. I don't know how I would've handled it if you had said no."

She laughs. "Like there was ever a chance for that."

"A man never knows until he hears that three-letter word."

"Yes. Yes. Yes," she says, kissing my chest between each one.

"So, are you ready for your next surprise?" My heart is beating double time, and she has to hear it, feel it, as she's still resting on my chest. I took a gamble with her next surprise, and I hope it was a good one.

"Yes," she says again.

Standing, I lace my fingers through hers. "Let's take a walk."

"It's dark. Do we need a flashlight?" she asks.

"Nah, it's fine."

She nuzzles into my chest as we walk through the wildflowers. There's a small path that's cut large enough for the Gator to get through, a trail we use not only for the Gator but for the horses to get down beside the big pond that's nestled in the back corner of the field.

"Where is that light coming from?" she asks, staring straight ahead.

"That's part of your other surprise."

"What did you do?" she asks, her voice full of happiness.

I can't help but feel like I should be standing a little taller, knowing I'm the reason for her happiness. "I had an idea, and well, I hope I didn't go too far."

At the top of the hill, there's no hiding the lights or where they're coming from.

"Is that a gazebo?" she asks.

"It is."

"You bought me a gazebo?"

"Well, I built it. Me and the guys."

"I wanna see it," she says, then takes off running down the hill, her laughter following her. I go after her and reach her just as she stops in front of the new gazebo, lit up with battery-operated lights.

"Wow," she breathes as I wrap my arms around her from behind.

I take in the scene before us, seeing what she sees. There are pink and white roses and wildflowers decorating the railing. Small strings of lights hang from the roof, giving off a romantic glow.

"You did all this?" she asks.

"I did."

"Thank you," she whispers.

"I had another idea."

"Oh, yeah? You seem to have a lot of good ideas this evening."

"Well, I was thinking we could get married here." She sucks in a breath, and I know she's picturing it in her mind. "Tomorrow," I add.

She immediately turns in my arms to face me.

"What did you just say?"

"Will you marry me? Here, tomorrow evening, just as the sun sets?"

She studies me. "You're serious?"

I nod. "I have the guest list, all of our closest friends and family, just like you wanted. I have the food, just as you asked, pulled pork barbecue and some sides. I have a small wedding cake, big enough to feed our guests and for us to have a small top tier for our one-year anniversary. I have a bouquet of wildflowers with pink and white roses. I have a pair of dark jeans with a button-down shirt, and my cowboy boots are already shined." I pull her closer, needing more of her. "Now," I say softly, "I have a fiancée, who I know has a dress. I even arranged for her hair and makeup to be done. Everything is all taken care of. I just need you to give me that three-letter word one more time tonight."

"Dave, I—" She stops and places her hands on my cheeks. "Yes."

One simple word causes my heart to beat so hard in my chest, I feel it may burst.

"I love you so fucking much." I press my lips to hers.

"It's bad luck to spend the night together before our wedding," she informs me.

"Yeah, that's the only bad part about this. I knew you would say that. You're staying here, in your old room. Jamie is coming to stay with you. In fact"—I look down at my watch—"she's probably already there, waiting on us."

"You did all of this?"

I nod. "You said to surprise you."

"You went all out." She smiles, her eyes still wet with tears.

"There is no other way for me to be when it comes to you."

"Do we have to go back right now?"

"We can stay out here as long as you want."

"Just a little longer. Will you dance with me?" she asks.

Pulling my phone from my pocket, I hand it to her. She unlocks it and scrolls through my music until I hear Brantley Gilbert singing again.

"This is our song," she says softly. With my phone still clutched in her hand, she wraps her arms around me and buries her face in my chest.

My phone chimes with a message, which has her moving away just as the song ends. Looking at the screen, she smiles before turning it to show me.

Jamie: You're killing us. Did she say yes?!

I throw my head back and laugh. "We'd better get back. Knowing Jamie, she'll have your brother drive her back here."

"I can see her doing just that."

She hands me my phone, and I send off a group text to our friends and parents.

Group text: She said yes!

I power off my phone before sliding it into my pocket. We'll see them soon enough.

15

Olivia

I wake to the moon shining through the window of my childhood bedroom. Lifting my head, I look over at the nightstand to see it's a little after 5:00 a.m. No way am I getting back to sleep.

Today is my wedding day.

I replay last night, the proposal, and then the news that our wedding is planned. He remembered every detail, and while some girls might be offended that they didn't get to do all the work, I'm relieved. Who needs the stress of the planning? I love the fact that Dave did that for me. For us. He took a gamble, sure, but my fiancé knows me all too well. He had to know I wouldn't be upset.

He followed my details to the letter, or that's what Jamie told me last night. Apparently, he typed it all out and passed out duties to our friends. They were all in on it, our parents, too. How could I be upset about having people who love me willing to go out of their way to make my wedding day everything I ever dreamed?

Grabbing my phone from the nightstand, I send David a message.

Me:	I miss you.
David:	Did you get any sleep at all?
Me:	Yeah, a few hours. Just woke up. You?
David:	Same. It's hard to sleep when you're not next to me.
Me:	We're taking care of that later today.
David:	That we are.
Me:	Thank you.
David:	For?
Me:	Loving me.

I see the bubbles pop up and then disappear, as if he were replying but changed his mind. Two seconds later, my phone vibrates, and his picture is smiling back at me.

"Hello," I whisper.

"Never thank me for loving you. Never thank me for something that is as easy as breathing."

My eyes well up with tears at his sweet words. "I love you."

"I know you do, baby. I love you, too. Today, you're going to give me a precious gift. In turn, I'll do the same."

"My heart," I murmur.

"Yeah, your heart for mine?" he asks.

"That's the best offer I've had in a while."

He chuckles softly. "You should try to get a few more hours of sleep."

"Can we change the time?" I ask him.

"Of the wedding?"

"Yeah, I know you picked sunset, but I was kinda hoping we could move it up."

"I thought you wanted sunset?"

"I thought I did, too. Turns out, I just want you to be my husband."

"Is that really what you want?"

"Yeah, I mean, if we can make it happen?"

"Let me call the photographers." He laughs.

"Oh, I think they'll be able to work us in a little earlier."

"Yeah, they're both pretty amazing. Gramps is marrying us, and our moms are taking care of the food. Let me make some calls in a couple of hours, and we'll make it happen."

"I wish you were here."

"Me too, Livy. Me too. Get some rest, beautiful. We've got a big day ahead of us."

"See you at the gazebo," I whisper.

"Damn right, you will."

Ending the call, I close my eyes and eventually drift back to sleep.

A few hours later, I wake to the sun shining through the windows and the smell of coffee. Climbing out of bed, I use the restroom, brush my teeth, and head downstairs. Jamie and my mom are sitting at the kitchen island with a list in front of them.

"Good morning, sleepyhead," Mom greets me.

"Morning." I fill a cup with coffee and take a seat next to them. "What are you looking at?"

"Just our list for today. Your fiancé called to tell us that we're moving the wedding up to five this evening."

I can feel my face heat. "Yeah, we talked at about five this morning and decided to move it up."

"You wanted sunset," Mom reminds me. She points to another list. "It says so right here."

I laugh. "I know, but it turns out, I just want to be married. Besides, I think the pictures with the wildflowers will do better in the early evening light."

"Have you been talking to McKinley and Whitney? They both said the same thing when David told them sunset." Jamie smiles.

"No, but they're right. It'll be better. At least that's what I'm hoping. So, what can I do to help?"

"Nothing," Mom answers. "We have it under control. You and Jamie are going into town to get your hair and makeup done. Nails, too, if you have time with the new schedule."

"You don't have to take me," I tell Jamie.

"Seriously? After everything you did for our wedding, this is the least I can do. Besides, I need a pedicure." She holds out her foot as if to prove her point.

"Thank you. What time do we go?"

"Two o'clock. I tried to change the time, but it's all booked."

"That's fine. I want to leave my hair down with some curls, so it should be easy enough. We'll be back in plenty of time."

"You know," Mom says, looking at me and then Jamie, "you two are the easiest brides I've ever encountered. Just going with the flow."

"All that matters at the end of the day is who you're marrying," I tell her.

"You've always talked about your perfect country wedding. You're not even a little disappointed?"

I think about her question. "No, not at all. I always thought it was the details of the day that made it the perfect wedding. I was wrong. It's the person you're sharing your life with. David is an amazing man who loves me, and I love him. At the end of that day, that's all that matters."

"Well said." Mom smiles. "Now, how about some breakfast?" She stands and pulls a prepared plate of food out of the microwave that she saved for me.

"Thank you." I waste no time digging in.

"After you eat, shower." Jamie looks at her phone for the time. "Then it'll be time for us to go."

"What time is it?" I ask.

"Noon."

I cough around the bite I just took. "Noon, seriously? I slept that late?"

"Well, when you call your fiancé in the middle of the night and tell him to move up your wedding, it's exhausting," Jamie teases.

"Holy shit! I'm getting married in five hours."

"You are, so eat up," Mom says, giving me a stern look, which I'm sure is for my use of profanity in her kitchen.

Scarfing down my food, I rush upstairs and take a long, hot shower. I shave twice—everywhere, just in case. By the time I'm done and my hair is dry, it's time to leave for the salon.

"You excited for today?" Jamie asks once we're in her car and on our way.

"I am. No nerves, just excitement. How are you feeling?"

"Good. No morning sickness yet, knock on wood."

"That's great news. My big brother taking good care of you?"

"You know he is," she replies, her voice softening at the mere mention of her husband.

We make small talk about the bar and how my brother hovers over her now that she's pregnant. "I'm not surprised. Evan was that way with both Walker and Beau, and look at Aaron with Whitney. That poor woman can't even go to the restroom without him walking with her."

"I get both sides. I mean, I know it's annoying as hell, but at the same time, anyone who has never been loved like that is missing out."

"I have to agree."

"You think David will be that way?"

"I'm sure." I laugh. "We are talking about the guy who used to propose to me at least once a week."

"True." She pulls into the salon. "Hey, Alice," we greet our stylist when we enter.

"Ladies, how are you? Olivia, congratulations. That man of yours did some serious planning."

"I know he did. He's one of a kind."

"That he is. Do you know how you want your hair?"

"I'll be over here with Mary," Jamie says, heading toward the pedicure chair.

"Yeah, I want to leave it down and add some curls. Simple yet elegant."

"You're making my job easy. We'll have you done in no time."

"Good, because we moved up the time," I tell her.

"You did what?" Wide-eyed, she laughs.

"Yeah, I didn't want to wait and thought the photos would be better for early evening. Dave made it happen."

"Of course, he did. That man would do anything for you."

Alice took my simple instructions of down and some curls to another level. My hair never looks like this when I curl it on my own. My makeup is subtle and flawless, and we opt to keep my nails bare, just a clear topcoat, same with my toes. This was all accomplished in two hours.

"I can't wait to see the pictures," Alice says, giving me a hug. "Congratulations."

"Thank you." Jamie and I wave and head out the door. Apparently, my mother already paid for both of our services. Everyone I love rallied around me and made this day perfect.

"We have an hour to get you into your dress," Jamie says as she pushes the speed limit outside of town, headed back to my parents' place.

"It's fine. He's not going anywhere. We need to get there in one piece."

"I was only going five over." She laughs.

"Yeah, but you're carrying precious cargo. Besides, I don't need my brother barking about how I let you speed to get me there on time. All I have to do is add my veil and get dressed. We're ten minutes away. We've got this."

"Wow, calm, cool, and collected."

"Just taking a page out of your book, sister dear."

When we get back to my parents', Mom is waiting for us on the front porch.

"Hurry and get on in here. We can't risk David seeing you."

"Is he here?" I ask, looking around.

"No, but he will be. Get your rear in here." She places her hand on my shoulder and ushers me in the door. "Your hair is gorgeous."

"Thanks, Mom."

"Now, upstairs. We need to get you ready."

Without complaint, I make my way up to my old room, where, sure enough, my dress and veil are laid out across the bed. Whitney and McKinley are in there taking photographs of it.

"Great, you're here. Give me your engagement ring." She holds out her hand, and I hesitate. "I'll give it right back," she tells me.

Reluctantly, I slide the ring off my finger and hand it over. She places it, as well as a diamond band and a larger silver band, on top of my dress and snaps a few pictures. Whitney is doing the same, except her angle is farther away as she stands by the door. I don't question them; I know they work magic with their images. I'm honored that my two best friends are here and documenting this special day for me.

Mom and Jamie help me slide into my dress while McKinley and Whitney take more photographs. Jamie secures my veil, and when I turn to face them, the four of them have tears in their eyes.

"Hey, none of that," I scold them. "I am not messing up Alice's masterpiece."

"Honey, you're beautiful," Mom says while my three best friends murmur their agreement.

"Now"—Jamie wipes at her eyes—"that man of yours has some things for you. She hands me a box. Slowly, I open the lid to find a stunning jeweled bracelet inside with a note.

> *Livy,*
>
> *This was my grandmother's. She wore it on her wedding day, and my mother on hers. This can be your something old? I can't wait to marry you.*
>
> *David*

"And this," McKinley says, handing me another small box.

Opening the lid, I see a blue garter and feel my face flush. It, too, has a note.

Livy,

This is selfish and purely for me. I can't wait to take this off you.

This is your something new and something blue.

David

"Now mine." Mom steps forward. Another box, this one smaller, with a tiny note folded inside.

Livy,

You have two something olds because we need to represent your family and mine as we join together as one. These earrings are what your mom wore the day she married your dad.

David

"He's killing me." I laugh as I swipe under my eyes. "We should've done this before I had my makeup done."

"We can patch you up, don't you worry," Jamie assures me.

"My turn." Whitney steps forward, handing me yet another small package. Inside is a jeweled hair comb that looks similar to the bracelet he gave me, again with a note.

Livy,

This is your something new. It matches the bracelet, which I'm sure you noticed. I got lucky with that. The girls assure me this will look great with your veil today. Can't wait to see for myself.

David

I hand the comb to Jamie, and she secures it in my hair. "Looks as though it was made into the veil," she comments.

"He really did think of everything," I say, dabbing at my face with a tissue, trying hard not to destroy my makeup.

"He did. He loves you," Mom assures me.

"I love him, too," I say, just as there's a knock at the door.

Mom opens it just a crack to see who's there, and in walks my future mother-in-law. "Oh, Olivia, you're beautiful," she says, giving me a hug. "I have something for you," she says when she pulls back. "David is getting this same information right now. "His father and I wanted to do something, but by the time we knew what was happening, everything was set and taken care of, so we decided to send you on your honeymoon. We know you both like low-key, so we got you a house on Lake Michigan for a week. I already cleared it with Mike, Evan, and Aaron, and you two are good to go. We'll keep Dixie at our place," she says.

"Thank you so much." I give her a huge hug. "This is perfect." When she pulls away, she wipes her eyes. "Thank you, all of you, for being here and making this day special."

"Knock, knock. You ladies ready?" my dad asks from outside the door.

"Come in," Mom yells.

"Oh," he says, his mouth hanging open. "You look… my little girl's a looker." He smiles. "You ready? It's five, and if I know David, he's going to be pacing until he sees you."

"Is he there already?"

"He is, as are the guests. You ready?"

"As I'll ever be."

With the help of Jamie and our mothers, I climb into the horse-drawn carriage, which was not part of the dream wedding, but I love it and am so glad he thought of it. McKinley and Whitney are snapping pictures left and right before climbing on the Gator and following us—I'm sure snapping more pictures.

This is really happening. I'm getting married.

16

David

I've looked over the small knoll at least fifty times in the last ten minutes. I know she's coming. She loves me. But that still does nothing to calm my nerves. It's been too long since I've seen her. The anticipation is killing me. Of seeing her in her dress. Knowing that today she becomes Mrs. David Johnson. I'm ready for it to happen.

When she called me this morning and asked if we could move up the time, I was more than happy to make the calls. Even five minutes sooner is good for me. I've been waiting for this moment, if I'm honest, from the moment we started dating. Without a doubt, I knew she was the girl I was going to marry. Now, here we are, and my dream is about to come true.

"You doing okay, son?" my grandpa asks.

"Yeah. Just ready," I tell him.

He chuckles. "We've all been there," he says, pointing to my dad and my three best friends. The only person missing is my future father-in-law, because he'll be walking my bride to me. I look again over the knoll, hoping to spot them. "It's the anticipation."

"Yeah, I can't wait to see her in her dress."

He gives me a knowing smile. Sure, I want to make love to her as my wife. I know that's what he's thinking. Might be creepy as fuck, but it's the truth all the same. "We've waited so long. I'm just… ready."

"Well, look over there." He points over my shoulder, and sure enough, my bride and her father are riding toward us on a horse-drawn carriage. We opted for our guests to sit on hay bales, covered in quilts. It was Mom's idea, and it was a great one. A hell of a lot easier than lugging chairs that would be wobbly on the uneven ground. We didn't want there to be a bride's side and a groom's side. Instead, I opted for all the bales to be together and for her to walk around them to get to me. That wasn't a detail she painted for me, so I improvised.

I watch as the carriage stops just on the edge of the backside of the hay bales. My father-in-law climbs out first, then holds his hand out for Livy. When she stands, I lose my breath. It's not until Gramps claps me on the shoulder and whispers, "Breathe" — something my body should know how to do without being told — that I suck in a deep breath.

She's stunning.

My bride.

My wife.

I shift my feet, antsy to rush to her, to grab her in my arms and kiss the hell out of her. Instead, I hold strong, clasping my hands together, resting them in front of me. I have to wait, just a few more minutes, if that. A few minutes for a lifetime — it's a deal I'll take.

When they make it within reaching distance, I can't help it. I hold my hand out for her, and she takes it. Her dad just laughs and shakes his head. He knows I love her; everyone does. I've never hidden the fact from anyone. My eyes are locked on hers, which are bright and smiling. I don't hear what Gramps says, nothing more than a mumble. Then I hear her dad speak up, but I don't comprehend any of it. All I see, all I hear is her. It's her sweet laughter that pulls me out of my trance.

"You ready to do this, handsome?" she asks me.

Looking around, I see her dad on the hay bale next to her mother and all eyes on us.

"Absolutely," I say, placing my arm around her waist and pulling her close. I kiss her temple, because I can't not. She's fucking gorgeous, and my lips need to be against her skin. Just a sample of what the next sixty-plus years are going to hold for us.

I told Gramps to keep things simple. It was another detail she didn't tell me about, but she did say simple yet elegant, so I thought simple worked in this case.

Traditional vows are said. I slide my ring onto her finger, saying, "I do," and she does the same.

It's an odd feeling. I'm here, but I'm not. I feel as though we're floating through time. I can't wrap my head around the fact that she's mine. My wife, my future, all mine.

"By the power vested in me by the state of Kentucky, I now pronounce you husband and wife. You may kiss your bride."

I hear the words and step forward slowly. I feel as though I missed most of it, that it's a fog, but this part I'm not going to miss. Cradling her face, I lower my mouth to hers, hovering just over her lips.

"I love you, Mrs. Johnson," I murmur before taking her lips with mine. I trace her lips with my tongue until she opens for me. It's not until I hear hollering and whistling that I know I've taken it too far. Pulling back, I rest my forehead against hers. "We did it, baby."

"We did it. I love you, husband."

"Say it again."

"I love you."

"Not that, the other thing."

She laughs, her smile infectious. "I love you, husband."

"Fuck, it feels good to hear you say that. I'll never get tired of hearing it. Never." I kiss her slowly and deeply. "I love you, too, wife."

I get it. Not that I didn't before, but now I truly understand why Mike refers to Jamie as his wife every damn chance he gets. It's liberating. One word shows the world that we're in this together. That the love we share runs deep.

"Yeah? Sixty or so years?" she asks.

"More. There will never be enough time with you." With one more quick kiss to her soft, plump lips, we turn to face our families. Hands welded together, we hold them in the air as they cheer for our union.

Whitney and McKinley drag us away for pictures. Then our parents and Mike and Jamie join us. They even let Evan and Aaron run the cameras to take pictures of all the girls together before taking back control and doing the same with the guys.

After photographs, my wife and I climb into the horse-drawn carriage and follow everyone on Gators and four-wheelers to the barn. We have tables set up and the pulled pork and sides, just as my wife suggested. I don't leave her alone, not for a single second, as we eat, dance, and cut the cake. Through all of it, I stay right by her side, where I plan to always be.

"Good day?" I ask her as I spin her around the makeshift dance floor in the barn.

"The best day."

"Everything you dreamed?"

"So much more. You, my husband, are so much more."

"What's our next step?"

Looking up at me, her eyes shine. "Babies?" she asks softly.

"Yeah?" Even I can hear the hope in my voice. I want nothing more than to start a family with her.

She nods. "When you're ready."

"So tonight?" I ask, making her laugh.

"Does that work for you?"

"Now works for me, but I have a feeling you would frown upon leaving this soon." My grip on her hips tightens. I want to throw her over my shoulder and rush off into the night to have my wicked way with her.

"You know me too well." She rests her head on my chest. "Are we really doing this?" she asks.

"Yeah, Livy, we're really doing this. You sure you're ready?"

"Yes."

One word, the one I love to hear from her.

"Then tonight." I kiss her softly and let everything and everyone fade into the background. My wife got her country wedding and me, a southern boy full of devotion for her.

epilogue

David
ten years later

It's hard to believe it's been ten years since the day I married the love of my life in a field of wildflowers on her parents' property. A lot has changed in ten years. Olivia and I have three beautiful kids, and even though I never thought it would be possible, I love her more each day. That's why I couldn't let our tenth anniversary pass by without a celebration. I just failed to tell my wife about it. Or my kids, really. Those little buggers can't keep a secret to save their lives.

Our son, Carson, is nine. He was born almost exactly one year to the day of our wedding. His birthday was two weeks ago. He's pumped that he's just a year away from double digits. He's got my brown eyes and Olivia's lighter brown hair. He loves soccer and being the protector of his little sister. He agrees with me that she can't date until she's thirty.

Our daughter, Crystal, just turned seven. She's a little spitfire, with her momma's spirit and big green eyes. Her hair is darker like mine. She's our little tomboy through and through. She wants to do everything her brother does, which drives Carson crazy. Lexi has tried countless times to let her do her hair and makeup, but my little girl just isn't having it. She idolizes her older brother.

Then we have our little man, Cade. He's four and my little mini-me; there's no denying it. We have the same dark brown hair and dark eyes. He follows his brother and sister around and gets angry when they do things he can't. He'll pass up anyone for his momma, and just like his brother and sister, he brings so much joy to our lives.

I tried without success to get Olivia to have another one. She said three was a good number. Although she said no more babies, we haven't given up practicing, you know, just in case one day, we change our minds.

I sent the little secret tellers to my parents' for the day. Olivia is at the tavern, doing inventory. The place is thriving, and she and Mike have a great system down. They alternate weekends for inventory, and they have a great staff, which allows them not to be there every night. Inventory only takes a couple of hours, so it's not a bad gig. That also means I have that amount of time to finish setting up for today.

I thought it would be good to bring us back to where it all started—the field of wildflowers. We've taken our kids there often, and of course, we've shown them photographs. I liked the idea of surprising my wife and our kids with an anniversary celebration at the exact spot. Mike, Evan, and Aaron are all on board and have promised not to tell their wives. Not that I think any of them would tell her, but these days, we have all kinds of little ears running around, and they pick up on everything. No doubt one of them would hear a conversation, and the surprise would be ruined. Better safe than sorry.

I did, however, need McKinley's and Whitney's services. I want today documented. With that in mind, I made sure the guys didn't let them make plans and to have them here at my in-laws' today at two.

I'm sitting on the front porch when Mike and Jamie pull up.

"Uncle Dave!" My niece and nephews come rushing over. Mike is the oldest at nine. He's going to be ten in a couple of months. Then we have Chase, who just turned eight, and sweet Ellie, who is three. To say my in-laws are over the moon with their six grandchildren is an understatement.

"Hey, guys." I gather the three of them in a hug. Little Miss Ellie climbs up on my lap and snuggles with me. She's my girl. My own little angel refuses to give me snuggles at the ripe old age of seven.

"You ready?" my brother-in-law asks me.

"Yeah, pretty much. Just need to hook the wagons up. I came over last night, telling Liv I had to help your dad, and got the hay on them. Evan and Aaron came over bright and early this morning and helped string the lights, and I picked up the flowers on the way here." I point to the Gator, the back overflowing with flowers. The exact same arrangement as our wedding day. "Your mom and mine took care of the food. Mine should be here any minute."

"What's going on?" Chase asks.

"We're having a party," I tell him.

"I wike parties," Ellie says, still snuggling against my chest.

"So, what's left?" he asks.

"Wait a minute," Jamie chimes in. "What kind of party? Why did I not know about this?"

"Well, I didn't want the cat to get out of the bag, so to speak. I'm throwing Liv a ten-year wedding anniversary party this afternoon. We're going to be in the same field with the same food and flowers."

"Aww," she says, then smacks her husband lightly on the arm. "You should have told me." He rubs his arm as if she hurt him, when we all know that's not the case. "I could have helped." She turns back to me.

"Well, I do need your help, actually. Can you call Whitney and McKinley, tell them we're all hanging out here today and to bring their cameras? Tell them you've been wanting to get some pictures of the kids."

"Why not just tell them the truth?"

"Too risky." I shake my head and laugh.

"Hey, we pulled off your wedding just fine," she challenges.

"You did," I agree. "But now we have a heck of a lot more munchkins running around, and I can't risk them overhearing."

"It's not nice to lie, Uncle Dave," Mikey, as we call him, reminds me.

"It's a surprise," I tell him. "It's not a lie when you're trying to surprise someone."

He looks over at his dad for confirmation, and Mike nods.

"Fine," Jamie grumbles, then pulls out her phone and starts making calls.

"What else?" Mike asks.

"Nothing really. Just waiting for everyone to show up. Liv should be at the tavern for at least another hour or so. My parents will be here with our kids and their portion of the food in about half an hour. When they get here, they're going to set it all up in the barn."

"Looks like you have it under control."

"Don't jinx me." I laugh as Jamie ends her call.

"Evan and McKinley are on their way. Evan spilled the beans this morning, so she was already in the know."

I throw my head back and laugh. He never could keep a secret from Kinley. "What about Aaron and Whitney?"

"Apparently, Kinley called Whit, and they're on their way, as well."

"Perfect."

"You should have told us," she says again, sliding her phone back into her pocket.

"I know. I'm sorry, but I really wanted to pull this off."

"I get it, I do. I just wish I were in on it." She smiles, letting me know she's not really upset with me.

"Well, you're in on it now."

She nods, her smile growing. "I'm going to go see if Grandma needs help. Ellie, you want to come with Mommy?" She holds her hand out for her daughter, but Ellie snuggles up to me, refusing to go. Mikey and Chase grab the basketball from the porch and start shooting hoops.

"Didn't take them long." Mike laughs as Aaron and Whitney pull in. Aaron helps Whit with her camera while their ten-year-old twin boys, Levi and Tate, rush over to play basketball.

"David Johnson," Whitney scolds me. "How dare you keep us out of the surprise."

I go through the same story I did with Jamie, and I can see her anger, which was actually more sadness than anything, slip away. "I just couldn't risk it," I tell her.

"Fine. I'm going inside to see if they need any help." Aaron kisses her cheek and then walks up the steps. She stops to say hi to Ellie, who gives her a toothy grin but stays in my arms.

"Round three," I say when I see Evan and McKinley pull up. Lexi, who is thirteen, soon to be fourteen, rushes to me, and Ellie goes to her immediately. They head inside to get a sucker. I like to think it's the sticky, sugary treat that tempted my niece away from me, though Lexi is a mother hen, and Ellie eats it up. Walker and Beau, who are now twelve and ten, join the rest of the boys playing basketball.

"Evan explained," McKinley says when I open my mouth to tell her why I kept them out of the loop. "But next time, include us. We're adults, David," she scolds.

"I know, but the risk and the reward." I offer her a smile. She just shakes her head and goes into the house.

I'm shooting the shit with the guys, watching the time. Just as I pull my phone out to call my parents, they pull in. Carson is out of the van and rushing to play basketball, with Crystal hot on his heels. Dad carries a sleeping Cade, Mom trailing behind him.

"I'll take him." I stand from my spot on the step and take my son. He's sweaty from sleep, but he doesn't move a muscle. He's out.

"Where do you want this food?" Mom asks.

"I'll take it over to the barn," Evan says, following her back to the van, with Aaron right behind him.

"What else needs to be done?" Dad asks me.

"We need to bring the food from inside over to the barn, and then we wait on Liv."

"She has no idea?" he asks.

"None at all. At least, if she does, she's hidden it really well." I know my wife, and if she even thought I might be planning something, she would have been asking questions, trying to be all nonchalant and failing miserably.

Cade stirs in my arms, and I rub his back to soothe him. I was scared as hell when Carson was born. A tiny little human who was my responsibility. It was up to me and Olivia to give him everything he needed. It took us a couple of weeks, but we got into a groove and never looked back. By the time Crystal came along, the only fear I had was being able to love another child the way I loved Carson. It was crazy and irrational, but real all the same, until we had our first ultrasound, and I realized my fear was unwarranted. I love all three of my kids with everything I am. If my wife were to ever be pregnant again, I would love that child just the same.

Mom comes over and takes Cade from me so I can help transfer all the food. Once we have it all done, the guys park their vehicles behind the barn and load everyone up on the hay wagon. Once they're gone, I call my wife.

"Hey, you. I'm just leaving."

"Great. I brought the kids over to your parents'."

"Really?" she asks, surprised.

"Yeah, your mom called and said she made cookies, so we stopped by." That's not a complete lie. My mother-in-law did make cookies for the kids. I, on the other hand, bought a small anniversary cake.

"Okay, well I'll just come there. Be there in ten."

"Be safe, babe." I hang up and text Mike, telling him she's on her way.

epilogue

Olivia

When I pull into Mom and Dad's, David is sitting on the front steps. I park behind his truck and climb out of my SUV. "Hey, you," I say.

He stands and meets me midway down the sidewalk, wrapping me in a hug and kissing the corner of my mouth. "How was your day?"

"Good. Where are the kids?"

"Oh, your mom and dad took them for a walk."

"Huh." It's not the craziest thing that's happened, but it's odd.

"Yeah, what do you say we hop on the Gator and drive back to our field?"

"Our field?" I ask.

"Yep. Ten years ago tomorrow, you promised me forever." He pulls me closer to him.

Resting my hands on his chest, I look up at him and wait until I have his full attention before saying, "I love you more today than I did that day."

"Look at you, getting all sweet and sentimental," he teases.

"You ruined the moment." I laugh when he tickles my side.

"Come on, wife, let's go take a look at where it all began."

"I should go say hi to the kids first." I try to step out of his hold, but he's got a tight grip.

"I love our munchkins, but if you do, they'll want to go. Come on, just me and you, for old times' sake."

He has a point. "Okay, I'll just send Mom a text." I reach for my phone that's in my back pocket and send off a text to my mom.

> **Me:** Dave and I are going to drive back to the wildflower field. Do you mind keeping an eye on the kids a little longer?

Her reply is immediate.

> **Mom:** Sure, honey. Take your time.

"She's good," I tell David.

"You knew she would be." He laces his fingers through mine and leads me to the Gator.

"You had this planned?" I ask him.

"Yeah, thought it would be nice to go back to where it all began."

"Babe, we've brought the kids back here more times than I can count."

"I know, but with tomorrow being our anniversary, I thought it would be nice for just us to visit here. Maybe do some of that kissing the kids are always saying grosses them out."

I throw my head back and laugh. "Carson will be so disappointed he missed it. Are you scarring our children for life?"

"Nope. He needs to know what it looks like to love someone so deeply that you can't go a day without kissing her. Same goes for Crystal. I want her to see how a man should treat her."

"You're amazing, David Johnson."

"Right back at you, Olivia Johnson."

The rest of the ride is peaceful, neither one of us needing to fill the quiet. We're just enjoying the ride and the time together.

When we get to the knoll, David slows down. Reaching over, he laces his fingers through mine and then creeps over the top of the hill. I'm watching him, wondering what's going through his head.

"Liv, look." He motions toward the bottom of the hill. I turn and gasp when I see all of our friends and family waiting for us.

As we get closer, they begin to clap and cheer. The kids jump up and down—all of them, not just ours.

"What is this?" I ask once we're stopped.

"It's our ten-year anniversary party. Same guest list, a few more kiddos, including our own, and minus one preacher."

"How did you…? When did you…?" I can't seem to form a complete sentence. "You did all this?" I'm finally able to push the words out of my mouth that make sense.

"Yeah, I had help." He points to our friends and family. "They all pitched in. I wanted this day to be special for you. Ten years, baby. You've been my wife for ten years. You've given me three beautiful babies and more happiness than one man should be lucky enough to have. I love you. Thank you for this incredible life we live."

Tears slide down my cheeks. I raise my hand to wipe them away, but he beats me to it. Gently, he cradles my face, using his thumbs to dry my cheeks. "Good surprise?" he questions.

"The best." I smile at him. "I didn't realize when I told you to surprise me ten years ago that you would be carrying on the tradition."

"It seemed like a good plan." He winks. "Now, let's go hug our babies and spend time with our family. Tonight, we celebrate just the two of us. Mom and Dad are taking the kids with them for a sleepover."

"Really?"

"Yep. You ready to start working on baby number four?"

"I'm not against practicing," I whisper against his lips before pressing mine to his.

"All right, you two, cut it out. There are kids present," Mike yells out.

Pulling back from the kiss, he holds my stare. "I sure am glad you gave this southern boy a chance. I love our life and can't wait to see what the next fifty-plus years hold for us."

"Of course, I did. What girl wouldn't give her heart to a southern boy who's devoted to her?"

"I wouldn't know. You're all I see."

Thank you so much for reading *Southern Devotion*.

Never miss a new release:
Visit my website and sign-up for my Newsletter.

Be the first to hear about free content, new releases, cover reveals, sales, and more.

Start the **Riggins Brothers Series** for FREE.
Download *Play by Play* now.
Start the **Kincaid Brothers Series** for FREE.
Download *Stay Always* now.

You can also find free reads and bonus content on my website.

KAYLEE RYAN

Website:

kayleeryan.com/

Facebook:

bit.ly/2C5DgdF

Instagram:

instagram.com/kaylee_ryan_author/

Reader Group:

bit.ly/2o0yWDx

Goodreads:

bit.ly/2HodJvx

BookBub:

bit.ly/2KulVvH

TikTok:

tiktok.com/@kayleeryanauthor

KAYLEE RYAN

also by

With You Series:

Anywhere with You | More with You | Everything with You

Soul Serenade Series:

Emphatic | Assured | Definite | Insistent

Southern Heart Series:

Southern Pleasure | Southern Desire
Southern Attraction | Southern Devotion

Unexpected Arrivals Series

Unexpected Reality | Unexpected Fight | Unexpected Fall
Unexpected Bond | Unexpected Odds

Riggins Brothers Series:

Play by Play | Layer by Layer | Piece by Piece
Kiss by Kiss | Touch by Touch | Beat by Beat

Out of Reach Series

Beyond the Bases | Beyond the Game
Beyond the Play | Beyond the Team

The Everlasting Ink Series

Does He Know? | Is This Love? | Are You Ready?
What About Now? | Can We Try?

Entangled Hearts Duet
Agony | Bliss

Kincaid Brothers Series:
Stay Always | Stay Over | Stay Forever
Stay Tonight | Stay Together | Stay Wild
Stay Present | Stay Anyway | Stay Real

Standalone Titles:
Tempting Tatum | Unwrapping Tatum | Levitate
Just Say When | I Just Want You
Reminding Avery
Hey, Whiskey
Pull You Through
Remedy | The Difference
Trust the Push | Forever After All
Misconception | Never with Me
Merry with Me

Cocky Hero Club
Lucky Bastard

Mason Creek Series
Perfect Embrace

The Kissing Games Series
Kissing the Rival

Co-written with Lacey Black:

Fair Lakes Series
It's Not Over | Just Getting Started | Can't Fight It

Standalone Titles
Boy Trouble | Home to You | Tell Me A Story

Never to Far Series
Beneath the Fallen Stars | Beneath the Desert Sun

There are so many people who are involved in the publishing process. I write the words, but I rely on my team of editors, proofreaders, and beta readers to help me make each book the best it can be.

Those mentioned above are not the only members of my team. I have photographers, models, cover designers, formatters, bloggers, graphic designers, author friends, my PA, and so many more. I could not do this without these people.

And then there are my readers. If you're reading this, thank you. Your support means everything. Thank you for spending your hard-earned money on my words and taking the time to read them. I appreciate you more than you know.

Special Thanks:

Becky Johnson, Hot Tree Editing.

Jaime Ryter Proofreading

Kari March Designs – Cover Design

Regina Wamba – Photographer

Tami - Formatting

Chasidy Renee – Personal Assistant

Jamie, Stacy, Lauren, Franci, and Erica

Bloggers, Bookstagrammers, and TikTokers

Lacey Black & Kelly Elliott

The entire Give Me Books Team

My fellow authors

My amazing readers